ENDURANCE

CLOVERDALE – BOOK THREE

BRUNO MILLER

ENDURANCE:
Cloverdale, Book Three

Copyright © 2019 Bruno Miller

Find out when Bruno's next book is coming out.
Join his mailing list for release news, sales, and the occasional survival tip. No spam ever.
http://brunomillerauthor.com/sign-up/

Published in the United States of America.

Would you fight for the ones you love?

The struggle for survival in Cloverdale continues as Vince Walker and a small group of survivors find that nothing comes easy in the post-apocalyptic ruins of what was once their town.

With a lack of emergency services and modern day conveniences, the reality of their situation forces them to rely on each other and become self-sufficient. Each new day brings with it a unique set of challenges that the group must rise above and conquer to eke out an existence.

Food, water and shelter aren't their only concerns, though. They must also defend themselves against an outlaw gang of looters determined to take control of the few resources that remain and kill anyone who gets in their way.

Will the survivors of Cloverdale stay united? Or will temptation divide them? How many will succumb to the evil that lurks in the shadows just beyond the town limits?

Other Books by Bruno Miller

The Dark Road Series

Breakdown

Escape

Resistance

Fallout

Extraction

Cloverdale Series

Impact

Survival

· 1 ·

Vince was still in disbelief about what had happened. How had he allowed himself and the others to be duped by the two travelers who had introduced themselves as Dave and Kelly from Indianapolis. Vince wasn't sure if he would ever stop beating himself up over the fact that he ignored his gut feeling about them.

Worst of all, they had taken Tom and Beverly's son, Ryan, hostage and were now using him as a bargaining chip. Vince and the others watched helplessly as Tom continued to stomp back and forth and shout threats about what he intended to do to the looters. Vince could hardly blame Tom for being angry and letting his emotions get the best of him, but they had to be smart about this, and chasing after Ryan without a solid plan wasn't the answer. Giving in to the looters' demands and turning over all their supplies wasn't an option, either, and would be suicide for their group. Vince meant what he said about rescuing Ryan without giving the looters what they wanted, but he didn't have a plan yet.

"Calm down, Tom. We'll figure this out," John tried, but Tom seemed to ignore him.

If Vince and the others were to survive this post-apocalyptic world, they would need all the supplies they could get their hands on. Vince's little group of thirteen was very lucky to have found the food at the grocery store and to have access to fresh water and sparing amounts of electricity. There were certainly others out there who were much less fortunate and who were managing to stay alive on less. But that didn't mean Vince wanted to join them in their struggle.

"If we don't give them what they want," Tom huffed, "they said we would never see Ryan again, and I believe them. I'm not willing to risk my son's life on some crazy plan."

Fred spoke up. "Well we can't give them all our stuff. We do that and we're as good as dead." Some of the others standing around the small circle nodded in agreement. Then Beverly stepped forward, rubbing her wrists. Vince noticed the red marks from the paracord and was surprised to see her suddenly composed and calm as she approached him and John.

"Then how do we get my boy back?" she asked solemnly.

"We take the fight to them. It's time to get proactive with these thugs," John said. Vince agreed, but how? They had no idea where the looters had taken Ryan or where they were based, although he figured they couldn't be staying too far from Cloverdale and he had seen them approach from the east the other day when he was at the quarry.

"If we're not going to give them what they want, then we're wasting time," Tom insisted. "Let's go after them now before they get too far."

"We will, but we need a plan," Vince said. "We can't go running off half-cocked and start another gunfight. We're running low on ammo, and it's too risky for Ryan's sake. Knowing them, they'll use him as a shield anyway." Vince tried to reason with Tom. Still, he knew it was easy to say these things but a whole lot different to be in Tom and Beverly's shoes. Vince could only imagine how he would feel if someone had taken Cy hostage. On top of all this, Ryan was just a kid and surely scared out of his mind right now. Tom was still worked up, and rightfully so, but they needed to have clear heads and think this through.

Tom, obviously unsatisfied with the answer, stormed off toward his motel room, grabbing Beverly's arm and dragging her along with him. He paused briefly and looked back at the group.

"I'm going to get my son. If anyone wants to do more than just talk about it, I'll be leaving in about fifteen minutes or as soon as I can get my stuff together. Don't try and stop me, either!" he snapped as he turned and started for the room once more. Following her husband, Beverly wore a look of hopelessness on her face. Vince couldn't help but feel that Tom's last comment was mostly directed at him, and he felt bad, maybe even a little responsible, for the situation they were in.

They needed to come up with some ideas fast or they were going to lose Tom and maybe Beverly if she went with him, not to mention that this situation had the potential to tear their group apart if he didn't do something soon.

"We can't let him go alone," Bill said.

"We're not," John answered, "but we can't go running off into the night without a plan. We need to be smart about this. These people won't hesitate to shoot any one of us or hurt the kid—I'm sure of it."

"John's right," Fred said. "We need to think this through. Let me go talk to Tom. Maybe I can get him to settle down a bit and buy us some time while you guys work something out." He turned and headed for the motel.

"I'll come with you and talk to Beverly." Hannah followed.

"How are we going to find them?" Cy asked. "We don't even know where they took Ryan." Vince was already thinking about that, and it was the biggest problem they faced. If they tried to catch up to the kidnappers, they would be seen or heard, and if they were spotted, the two imposters might try to hurt the kid in retaliation. Besides, there was a good chance that the two imposters had hooked up with the looters in the cars and fled together. They were probably long gone by now.

"Buster." Reese stepped forward from the shadows. She hadn't said a word since they gathered, and Vince had all but forgotten she was even there.

"What about Buster?" Vince asked.

"I did some training with Buster during the summers when I was home. We've done more than a few search-and-rescue drills with the volunteer fire department and the SAR—the search and rescue team. Buster can track scents pretty well. It started out as a sort of project for school and a paper I was writing, but he did so well at it that they asked us back every time they did training. He can track a piece of clothing or something from the person you're looking for up to twenty-four hours after an event. Buster and I helped find a little girl that was lost in the woods last summer over at Leiber State Park."

Vince and John looked at each other, then back at Reese.

"This could get dangerous," John said. "These people are armed and mean business."

"I know," Reese said, "but what other choice do you have? We can help."

"I can take Buster so you don't have to go along," Cy offered.

Reese shrugged. "It doesn't really work that way. I'm his handler, and we work together as a team. Buster won't respond as well to someone else, and I'm not even sure he'll do it with anyone other than me. That's just how it's done."

Vince didn't like the thought of taking Reese with them. The father in him was worried about her safety, but the pragmatist in him knew it was the only way it would work. He was skeptical about the dog being able to pick up the trail to begin with, but if having Reese lead the way would increase the odds, he was all for it.

The biggest question Vince had was, who was going to stay behind? Vince had considered that the looters' scheme could possibly have two parts to it. What if they were counting on Vince and the others to chase after them and leave their supplies unguarded and free for the taking?

There would be no talking Tom out of going along; that was one thing Vince was certain about. He just hoped Tom could keep a cool head when it came time to confront the kidnappers. They couldn't afford to have any loose cannons in the rescue party. This was going to be a team effort, and any rogue actions could put everyone's life in danger.

They really had no idea what they were up against or how many looters there were, but regardless of how big their rescue team was, Vince knew they would be outnumbered. This would have to be a stealth mission. Slipping into the looters' camp, or wherever they were holed up, unnoticed would be the only way this would work. And the more Vince thought it over, the more he favored letting the situation cool down a little before they headed out.

If they held off for a little while, maybe the looters would think their extortion and kidnapping plan had worked and that Vince and the others had decided to cooperate and hand over their supplies in exchange for the boy. If the looters were confident in their plan, they just might let their guard down. Maybe they would even celebrate their success and overindulge in drinking tonight. Waiting to take action was risky, but Vince didn't think the looters would harm the boy, not as long as they thought he was a bargaining chip.

If only he could convince the others to go along with this idea of letting things cool down before going after Ryan. He didn't really think anyone would object, except Tom. It would be a hard pill for Tom to swallow, and Vince was sure it would go against every fatherly instinct the man had, but it was their best chance at getting Ryan back alive.

· 2 ·

Vince explained his idea to the others, and they all agreed that as long as Reese was confident that a couple of hours wouldn't hinder Buster's ability to pick up the trail, then they should let things settle down first. Vince, Cy, John, Tom, and of course Reese and Buster would make up the rescue team. It took some convincing on Reese's part to get her parents to let her go, but she was firm and they realized the rescue had little chance of succeeding, or even beginning, without her and Buster.

Fred was able to talk some sense into Tom, and when Vince and John explained the reasoning behind their idea to wait before pursuing the looters, he eventually gave in to better judgment and calmed down. Vince still had some reservations about Tom's emotional health, but there was no talking him out of going along.

When everyone had retreated to the motel to gear up and load backpacks with water and food,

Vince stopped at each room to check in on the team members and make sure they were all packing the appropriate supplies. They needed to plan for the worst, which meant bringing not only food and water but plenty of ammunition as well.

Vince checked on Reese first and made sure she was comfortable carrying the 12-gauge shotgun they had taken off one of the looters. He was careful to go over the operation and proper handling of the gun and made her repeat the information back to him. It was a sad excuse for a crash course in gun safety, but there was no time for anything more elaborate and he wanted her to be armed.

A sense of guilt loomed over him like a dark cloud as he felt the disapproving stares of Reese's parents. He didn't like taking her along any more than they did, and he promised he wouldn't let anything happen to their daughter. He tried to downplay the gun as nothing more than a safety precaution, a "just in case scenario," but he didn't think anyone was buying it. He sure wasn't, and the chance that she would have to use it was high.

Next, he stopped at Tom and Beverly's room. Vince found it difficult to knock on their door, but he forced himself to get it over with. Tom answered while Beverly remained inside, unmoving and kneeling on the floor by the bed. Vince could hear her whispers as she prayed quietly into her hands, only pausing occasionally to wipe the tears from her eyes. Tom came outside to talk and slowly closed the door behind him.

"She's taking it pretty hard," Tom said. "To tell you the truth, I'm not sure how I'm still standing here. This whole thing is eatin' me up inside, Major."

"I know it is, Tom, but you have to trust me and have faith in what we're doing. It's the safest way to go about getting Ryan back. If we go chasing after them, it's likely to become a hostage situation and a standoff with your boy in the middle. This is the only way to do it."

Tom shook his head and looked to be on the verge of tears. "It's hard to sit here knowing my son is out there, alone and scared."

Vince put his hand on Tom's shoulder. "I know, but trust me, we're going to get him back. Failure isn't an option, and none of us are willing to accept anything less than getting Ryan back here safe and sound ASAP." Vince tried his best to be convincing, but they were only words to the ears of a desperate man. Tom nodded but remained silent as Vince pulled out two thirty-round magazines for Tom's AR-15 from his back pocket.

"John wanted me to give you these for the trip. He's bringing a few more boxes as well. Don't forget to bring food and water. Enough for Ryan, too. It may be a ways away, and we'll all need to keep our energy levels up to get back." Vince hoped that ending on a positive note would provide Tom with some much-needed encouragement, but the look on his face remained unchanged as he nodded and sank back through the doorway. Vince glanced over his shoulder and saw Beverly in the same position as before, hunched over the bed and praying.

As Tom closed the door, Vince moved down the corridor to Cy's room, thinking about the grim conversation that Tom and his wife were having right now and how he wouldn't have wished this on his worst enemy. He could only imagine how helpless they felt, not to mention the whirlwind of other emotions running through their minds.

When he reached Cy's room, the door was partially open. John was inside, talking with Cy and giving him several boxes of ammunition for his AR-15. The two looked up at Vince as he entered the room.

"You guys ready for this?" Vince directed the question primarily at his son.

"Yep. John's just giving me a little extra ammo to pack. We might need it." Cy said it so casually that Vince was caught off guard. For a moment, he wondered if Cy really grasped the severity of the situation. But how could he not? He had seen for himself what these people were capable of. In fact, Vince was beginning to feel foolish for calling them looters; in his mind, the word was far too kind for them. This human trash they were dealing with was nothing short of a band of murderous thieves and now kidnappers. They were a roving gang of bandits, plain and simple.

"Everybody still good to leave here at midnight?" John said, interrupting Vince's thoughts.

"Yeah," Vince said. "I just checked in on the others. Everyone is good to go. Looks like you guys have things under control here, so I might try to get a little rest before we leave." He checked his watch. "It's gonna be a long night."

"Yep, I'm planning on doing the same," John replied. "I'm all packed up and ready to go."

"All right then. I'll see you guys in the parking lot at twelve." Vince nodded and backed out of the room, leaving the door how he found it.

When he entered his room, Mary was lying on the bed and struggling to read a book in the dim light of a lantern on the nightstand. Nugget was curled up by her side, but at the sight of Vince, the little dog popped up and ran to greet him. Mary looked up and forced a smile as Vince plopped into a chair near the window and began to take off his boots. Before he could undo his laces, Nugget had wriggled her way between his legs and was demanding his attention. Vince scratched her all over, and she returned his affection with a few licks and nibbles to his hands.

Satisfied, Nugget leaped back onto the bed and

curled up into a ball once more, watching Vince take off his boots.

"Why don't you turn the lantern up a little more. It looks like you're having trouble seeing," Vince said.

"Oh, it's okay. I've been on the same page for the last five minutes anyway. I can't really concentrate." Mary sat upright on the edge of the bed and set the book on the nightstand. "Can't stop thinking about things, you know?"

"Yeah, I know." Vince sighed as he rubbed his hand over his gray beard and forced himself to his feet. He began to pack his bag, making sure to distribute the load for comfort by putting the heavier ammunition for the shotgun and his .45 along the sides and the water bottles at the bottom. A few energy bars went on top. Vince paused for a minute, looking around the room and wondering what else he should bring along.

"How long do you think you'll be gone?" Mary asked.

Vince shrugged. "Hard to say, really. I imagine we've got at least a few miles ahead of us. And who knows what we'll find when we get there. I just hope Buster can locate the trail and track them back to their camp."

"Well, Reese seems to think he'll be able to do it, no problem."

"I hope she's right." Vince stuffed a few headlamps into the top pocket of the backpack and zipped it up before setting the bag and his shotgun by the door. If he could help it, he didn't want to wake Mary up when he left. Depending on how long Vince and the others were gone, the group that stayed behind might have to stand watch more often and at the very least help out more tomorrow.

At any rate, he couldn't imagine they would make it back before dawn, and when they did return, they would all be thoroughly exhausted. So much for accomplishing anything of significance on his to-do list tomorrow. He shook the thought from his mind and tried not to think about everything he wanted to do. He was getting ahead of himself and needed to focus on the rescue.

"I'm going to try and rest a little here before we head out." Vince lay down on the bed opposite Mary and turned onto his side, trying to find a position that didn't bother his aching back. Moments later, he felt Mary's hand rubbing his shoulders and then the small of his back.

"Your back is hurting again, isn't it?" she asked.

"Yeah, it's not too bad. I just took something for it a little while ago." He did his best to downplay it, but it was hurting pretty badly. She must have known, because she kept rubbing until he fell asleep.

· 3 ·

"Dad... Dad, it's time to go. Come on, everybody's waiting." Vince slowly came to at the sound of Cy's voice. He squinted as he tried to look at his son standing in the doorway, but he couldn't make out his face due to the glare from Cy's headlamp.

"Okay, okay, I'm up. I'll be right out." Cy quietly backed out of the room and disappeared as Vince began to get up. Mary had fallen asleep next to him. He carefully rolled over to the edge of the bed, trying not to wake her. Sliding over to the chair by the window, he blindly reached for his boots in the darkness. Nugget's head shot up, and the little dog gave him a puzzled look before she took Vince's spot next to Mary and lay back down.

"Lucky dog," Vince whispered. He rubbed his face and tried to summon what little energy he had. Glancing at his watch, he realized that it was a little past twelve and that he had in fact overslept. A little bit of rest would pay off in the long run, but he was regretting it right now; it felt like he had only just finished packing his bag and lain down on the bed a couple of minutes ago.

Once his boots were laced up, he stood slowly and stretched, wincing as his back muscles tightened. He grabbed two pills off the table and washed them down with a glass of room-temperature water left over from last night. What he wouldn't give for a cup of coffee right now, but he was already late and the others were apparently waiting on him. Even if there was time, he wouldn't want to risk waking Mary up.

He grabbed his shotgun and backpack and snuck out. Nugget threw him one last bothered look as he closed the door. Cy wasn't kidding: they were all waiting, and Vince immediately felt guilty for oversleeping.

"Sorry about that, guys." Vince quickened his pace and joined the others around the hood of the pickup truck. Bill was standing watch and had just relieved Fred, who was still hanging around and talking with the group as Vince approached. Buster trotted over to Vince as soon as he spotted him. Vince rubbed his head and looked him over, wondering if this big happy-go-lucky dog was up for the task ahead.

Cy turned to his dad and offered him a steaming

cup of coffee. "Here you go. It's pretty strong, but it'll get you moving."

Eyes widening, Vince set his bag on the ground and took the cup. "Thanks, I could really use that." The coffee was strong, but he wouldn't have wanted it any other way. It was just what he needed to fully come around and get into the game.

"Nice of you to join us, Major," John teased.

"Moving a little slow this morning, if you can call it that," Vince said, glancing at his watch. He noticed the backpacks Dave and Kelly had carried were sitting on the hood of the truck.

"I see you went and got their bags," Vince said.

"Yeah," Cy answered, "I ran out and grabbed them. Reese thinks it's best for Buster to go off one of their scents."

"That's right," Reese said. "Buster will have a better chance of picking up their trail since they were carrying Ryan when they left. Plus, I can take something of theirs with us to give Buster what's called a scent article. They were both pretty sweaty, so these packs should have a good amount of smell to them." Reese approached the closest bag and unzipped it, then dumped its contents onto the hood of the truck. Vince wasn't surprised to see an assortment of rags and old bricks tumble out. He shook his head as he thought again about how they had fallen for the story hook, line, and sinker. It made him feel foolish but also hardened his resolve. Vince wanted retribution, and he was going to get it one way or another.

"So much for canned goods and clothes." John shot Vince a disgusted look. He looked as irritated as Vince felt about the whole thing.

"No matter. We'll use a piece of the bag itself." Reese produced a small pocket knife and proceeded to cut off a piece of fabric from the back area and placed it in a ziplock bag.

"Well, that ought to do it," Reese declared. "We're ready to go when you are."

Everyone glanced at each other before shouldering their bags and picking up their guns.

"Oh, I almost forgot." Vince leaned his gun against the truck and set what was left of his coffee down. He unzipped his backpack and pulled out a handful of headlamps.

"These all have a red LED setting. I suggest we use these to conserve our night vision. It will also make us less visible when we get close. Help yourselves." Vince tossed the pile of headlamps on the hood.

"We should start around back. That's the way they left," Reese said.

"Well, what are we waiting for? Let's get going." Tom fastened the headlamp and turned it on.

"We're right behind you, Reese. Lead the way," Vince said as he picked up his gun and slung on his bag. He and the small group made their way around the side of the motel and stopped when they reached the back door that led out of the kitchen.

"This is where we start. Buster," Reese commanded. "Heel up. Heel up, boy."

Vince was somewhat shocked to see Buster's reaction; in a matter of seconds, the otherwise carefree dog perked up and ran to Reese's side, where he sat down a few inches from her right leg and waited astutely for his next command.

Reese opened the ziplock bag with the piece of backpack and presented it to Buster. He stuck his nose in the bag and sniffed at the scrap of cloth for a second or two, fogging up the plastic in the process. Reese closed the bag and stuffed it in her pocket, then gave Buster his next command. "Search! Come on, boy, you can do it. Search!" she said sharply.

Frozen in what seemed like a trance, Buster stared blankly at the trees. As Buster processed the command, Vince wondered if this was really going to work. What were they thinking? Had they actually put all their hopes into a dog's ability to find Ryan? He bit his tongue and remained quiet, patiently waiting for Reese and Buster to do their thing.

All at once, Buster launched from his heeled position and began sniffing the ground with a determination and seriousness that Vince would have never guessed he was capable of. Buster started making tight circles around the group, working his way farther out as he went. Then, just as quickly as he'd started, Buster stopped and sat down with his snoot in the air and looked back at Reese.

"He's got it!" Reese ran over and praised Buster with heavy scratching and a few pieces of food from her pocket before she stepped back and gave the next command. "Find! Find!" She pointed toward the woods behind the motel. There was no hesitation this time: Buster jumped up and headed off on the trail.

Vince was glad to see the dog spring into action, and for the first time since they had come up with this plan, he began to believe that it might actually work. Everybody fell into a single-file line behind Reese as she followed Buster into the sparse pines that grew just beyond the motel. Vince glanced over at the freshly disturbed pile of earth at the edge of the woods where they had buried Jim the other day. A few of the others looked in that direction as well. While Jim's death was sad, Vince hoped it would serve as a reminder of the type of people they were up against, although he doubted anyone needed reminding.

Buster began a pattern of running twenty to thirty yards ahead of the group before stopping to wait impatiently for Reese and the others to catch up. His big pink tongue hanging from the side of his mouth, he panted and sniffed at the air.

Vince noticed that the route Buster was leading them along had started to turn west and head back toward the road. Vince suspected that the kidnappers had circled around and made their way out to the highway, where they must have met up with the rest of their gang at some predetermined rendezvous point on the road beyond town.

Undoubtedly, the same looters who had pinned down Vince and John in the gunfight were also the ones who gave the imposters a ride back to their base of operations. Vince guessed that the two cars had never intended on coming into town or trying to force their way past the roadblock to begin with. Their sole purpose was to cause a distraction while their two accomplices played the part of weary travelers until they could grab a hostage. Vince was mad and a little embarrassed that they had fallen for the cheap trick, but he had to admit that a part of him was impressed by the scheme and the looters' ability to pull it off. He would never underestimate them again. It was a hard lesson, and he wouldn't forget it anytime soon. It would also be a very long time before he trusted any strangers who came through Cloverdale, and he was sure the others felt the same way. From now on, he vowed to listen to his gut whether it offended anyone or not.

· 4 ·

Vince's suspicions were correct, and after about ten minutes of walking, they emerged from the woods. One by one, they crossed the ditch and gathered at a spot just past the roadblock.

"Well, we didn't get very far," Tom said, but Vince and John were already headed over to where the looters' vehicles were parked during the firefight. Vince scanned the ground for shell casings and noticed the amount of brass on the ground.

"They used a fair amount of ammo." John reached down, picked up an empty casing, and inspected it closely before tossing it to Vince. John shook his head. "No wonder they were punching through the cars so easy."

Vince looked at the casing and strained to read the writing around the primer in the red glow of his headlamp. "It's a .300 Win Mag," he mumbled, glancing back at the roadblock. He could just barely make out the outline of the two cars he had pushed together with the loader. At this range, a .300 Winchester Magnum would have no problem penetrating both sides of the car, as they had seen; he and John were lucky to be alive.

Tom, Cy, and Reese joined them as Buster sniffed the ground. Vince saw the tire tracks where the two cars had peeled out in the grass.

"They were definitely here," Reese said as she watched Buster circle the area and confirm they were still on the trail.

"Man, they went through a lot of ammo," Cy remarked.

"Maybe they're running low." Tom stood, looking at the spent casings on the ground. And there were plenty to look at—at least a hundred littering the area—but Vince doubted they were running low. If they were, they wouldn't have been so careless.

"Or maybe they have plenty and aren't worried about it at all," Vince huffed. Either way, it was time to keep moving and Buster was growing restless. He had picked up the scent, which headed north toward the quarry, and was whining and pacing back and forth in an attempt to get Reese to follow him.

"But if they're traveling by car, how will he track them from here?" Tom asked.

Reese patted Buster on the head. "Scent can blow off of a person a lot like pollen off a flower and settle on nearby plants or objects. I know it sounds a little farfetched, but it's true. Buster can do it. I know he can." She started moving toward Buster. The dog took her cue and immediately resumed the hunt.

Vince admired her resolve, and before Tom could cast any more doubt about Buster's abilities, he followed Reese's lead and headed out. One by one, the others fell in line behind him, and they continued on.

They walked along the shoulder of the road and watched Buster do his thing. He constantly ran from one spot to the next along the road and the edge of the taller vegetation that bordered the woods. Occasionally, he would stop altogether like he'd lost the trail, then backtrack a few feet, sniffing and snorting at the ground until he found what he wanted.

It was hot outside, in Vince's opinion, at least for the time. It was close to 1:00 a.m., and he'd hoped it would be a little cooler for the bulk of their journey, but the temperature hadn't dropped much from the daytime. In fact, it was hot pretty much all the time now. That was one thing he couldn't help but notice since the bombs, and he was sure they were related, although he didn't understand the science behind it. The air felt bottled and stale, like they were trapped in a container with a tight lid. The absence of any breeze only added to his discomfort and seemed to exaggerate the heat rising from the asphalt.

Vince thought back to when he was a kid and would borrow an old mason jar from his mother to catch bugs around the farm. He was always careful to poke holes in the top so as not to kill whatever critter he had captured. He forgot to do that once while heeding his mother's call to come in and eat lunch, and when he returned, the grasshopper he'd trapped was dead. He felt like the forgotten grasshopper now.

What he wouldn't give for a good rain shower or thunderstorm to clear the air and give everything a much-needed rinse—him included. But at least they weren't fighting their way through the woods now that the scent had led them out onto the road. And Vince was grateful for that. He reminded himself it could be worse and wiped another bead of sweat from his brow.

They moved on in silence, each person following their own red spotlight on the ground in front of them. Vince had suggested everyone pivot their headlamps toward the ground and keep them there. Even though the red LEDs were the least visible form of light, he didn't want to chance being spotted. And every time he looked up and scanned his surroundings, he held his hand over the LED just in case.

For the most part they traveled in silence,

everyone dealing with the heat and misery in their own way. Other than their heavy footsteps on the pavement, the only sound was Reese's voice as she called out words of praise and encouragement to Buster every so often. The dog never seemed to slow his pace or waver in his determination, and Vince was beyond impressed with the smoothness of their teamwork. They had both far surpassed his expectations. Buster constantly checked back with Reese for approval, but only for a brief moment; then he returned to the task of tracking the looters.

As they passed the area beyond the overpass, where they had encountered the looters on their way back from the quarry, Vince noticed everyone but Reese looking over at the wrecked ATVs. He wondered if they were searching for the bodies like he was. He didn't see them, but it was dark. Or maybe the other gang members had retrieved them. Either way, he was glad to pass the area where Cy had rammed the car with the loader and even more pleased that no one had brought the incident up.

After another fifteen minutes or so of walking, they reached the four-way intersection with the westbound road that led to the quarry. They all stopped and looked around as Buster took in a few deep breaths of air. It was a good spot to stop and drink some water, and they all took a moment to do just that. From her bag Reese pulled out a plastic container that she had cut down to make a bowl and poured Buster some water before taking a drink herself.

Vince thought about how the two-way radio hadn't worked from this distance when they were getting the loader from the quarry, and he wondered if it would still yield the same result now. John's radios were high-quality units and should have covered this range with ease. From here, the motel couldn't have been more than a few miles away. The failure they experienced with the radios last time was another thing Vince chalked up to residual interference from the EMPs; at least that was his uneducated guess as to why they couldn't make contact at this short distance. Maybe that would improve with time.

"Hey, John, you want to see if you can reach Bill?" Vince asked.

John finished drinking and pulled the radio off his belt. "Good idea. Come in, Bill. Do you copy? Over." He fiddled with a few of the knobs as they all waited for a response.

"Yeah, go ahead. This is Bill. Over." There was a fair amount of static mixed in with Bill's voice, but they could hear him.

"Just doing a radio check. Over," John answered.

"Okay. A little bit of static on my end, but I can hear you clear enough. Over."

"Roger that. Same here. Over and out." John

was about to clip the radio back onto his belt when it crackled again.

"How are you guys makin' out? Over."

John glanced at Reese. "Buster's earning his keep. We'll check in later. Over."

"Copy that. Over and out." This time the radio stayed silent as John clipped it back onto his belt and turned the volume down. Vince was pleased to know the radios were working and they provided a small sense of security. It would be a good idea to check in from time to time as they traveled farther away. The signal was weak and most likely wouldn't improve. He guessed they would eventually stop working again, and it would be important to know at what point they lost communication with the others. Still, knowing they had backup if they needed it made him feel better.

Vince also brought along a flare in his bag, and they had agreed to only launch it in case of an emergency. If the flare went off, whoever was on watch was to come immediately with the truck. It wouldn't be much use once the sun came up, but at night, it could prove more reliable than the radio.

Buster seemed anxious to continue and began to lead them north in the opposite direction of the quarry. This came as no surprise to Vince and probably not the others, either. That was the direction the looters had come from the other night when Vince spotted the lights from the quarry. Just how far down this road was anybody's guess.

Tom shook his head. "I knew it."

"Yeah, let's just hope it's not too far." John wiped his face with a rag and stuffed it into his back pocket.

"What happens if we run into them out here? I mean, if we see them coming?" Cy asked.

"Then we get off the road and stay out of sight until they pass," Vince said. "They're not going back to Cloverdale tonight. They have what they came for and won't risk another fight if they think they're getting what they want tomorrow."

"I agree. We let them pass unless it's one vehicle. Then maybe we try to take them out," John said.

Vince nodded and was about to say he agreed, but Tom spoke up first. "As long as they don't have Ryan with them, I say we hit them with everything we have."

"We'll play it by ear, then." John turned to look at the others. "But first we get off the road and hide."

Everyone agreed, and the group started down the road with Buster and Reese in the lead once more. Based on Tom's outburst back there, Vince was a little concerned that even after they had Ryan in their possession, Tom might not be satisfied. He was clearly eager to exact justice on the looters, and while Vince understood his motivation, it worried him. Tom was clearly consumed by thoughts of revenge, and acting on his impulses could put them all in danger. They would have to keep a close eye on Tom.

· 5 ·

Reese was proud of Buster, and he had exceeded her expectations. They had participated in several drills with the Cloverdale Fire Department and specifically their SAR team, but the stakes had never been this high before. There was a lot of pressure for Buster to perform, and she didn't want to let anyone down.

Looking for a lost child in the woods was one thing; now, not only were they searching for a kidnap victim, but they were also dealing with some nasty people on the other end. It wasn't just Ryan who was in danger, and if they couldn't find him and bring him home, they would all be in trouble. On top of everything else, they were working against the clock.

She and Buster had been under time constraints before with the lost girl at Leiber State Park last year, but that was different. The worst-case scenario for the girl would have been spending the night alone in the woods. But Ryan wasn't lost; he'd been taken and was being held captive by a group of people who'd proven they would stoop to whatever level necessary to get what they wanted. They were killers, and this wasn't a game or a drill. This was the real deal, and it was up to Buster and her to find Ryan as soon as they could.

If they didn't get Ryan back by tomorrow night, the people who took him would expect the supplies to be waiting under the overpass by the interstate. And if everyone at the motel had to surrender their food and gear, how would she and the others survive?

Not that she thought the Major or John were the type to give in that easily. In fact, she was sure they wouldn't give in to the gang's demands, which meant there would undoubtedly be another fight. Either way, they were going to have to face these bad people again—there was never any doubt about that. Fighting with the looters seemed like the only certain thing in their future anymore.

That was probably what bothered Reese the most. She understood that the world was a different place now and that things would never be the same again. She'd even somewhat come to terms with the fact that she would most likely never see her friends again. But she couldn't stop thinking about when the next attack would happen.

In fact, thinking about the looters kept her up at night, when she waited to hear the warning sound of the truck horn. She tried not to let it bother her, but she couldn't shake the feeling of dread, and it was starting to affect her mentally. The lack of sleep alone made her feel like a zombie most days.

"Good boy. That's it. You're doing a great job, Buster." Reese praised her dog quietly as he raced off ahead with his nose in the air. She looked back to see how the others were doing and made eye contact with Vince, who shot her a quick smile and a nod of approval. Providing value to the group made her feel good, and she was glad that she and Buster could help out in such a big way.

She wiped the sweat from her face and followed after Buster, who continued darting back and forth from the bushes along the edge of the road to the hard-packed shoulder. Using the road was much easier than cutting a trail through the woods, but it was still hard work. The heat was relentless, and the lack of wind—or any movement for that matter—only added to their misery.

Reese hoped they could find Ryan tonight and make it back to the motel before the sun came up. Just the thought of being out in the heat of the day made her reach for her water bottle and take a long drink.

"Buster, you want some water? Water, Buster?"

Reese shook her bottle for the dog, but he seemed uninterested at the moment and stayed on task.

Just then, Cy picked up his pace until he was walking next to her.

"How's it going?" he asked.

"So far so good. He's still on the scent, doing what he does."

"We might have to take a break soon." Cy lowered his voice. "You know, for the old guys." He glanced over his shoulder.

"Yeah, I was wondering about that," she added with a smile.

"I know they won't say anything, but I think they might need a couple minutes to rest. We've been walking for over an hour now." Cy wiped the back of his neck with a cloth.

"I wonder how much farther we'll have to go to find them," she asked.

Cy shrugged. "I don't know. Let's hope not much."

Reese heard John try for a radio check with Bill. He tried several times but couldn't reach him. The rest of the group came to a halt as he continued trying.

John shook his head and looked at Vince. "I don't get it. We can't be more than five or six miles away. I should be able to reach him without any trouble."

"Yeah," Vince said. "I don't know why they're not working, either. My guess is the EMPs did something to the atmosphere. Must be causing some kind of interference, but what do I know?"

"We might as well take a breather here for a few minutes," John said.

"I can keep going. I'm good." Tom moved to the front of the group and looked ready to continue.

"We need to pace ourselves or we won't be worth anything when we find them," Vince reasoned.

"Just give us five minutes, Tom," John argued. "It's hot and we need to stay hydrated." Buster trotted back to the group and joined them. He nudged Reese's hand with his nose as she took a drink from her water bottle.

"Ready for that drink now?" She looked down at Buster as he panted loudly.

"That's a pretty good dog you've got there, young lady," John said. "I know I'm impressed."

"Thanks. He's a good boy. Aren't you?" Reese scratched Buster as he looked up from his makeshift water bowl, slobber trailing out from both sides of his mouth.

They all stayed there for a few more minutes without saying much of anything else. They were all tired; at least Reese figured they had to be. The big 12-gauge shotgun Vince and John insisted she carry was starting to feel heavy. While she understood the necessity of having the gun, it didn't make walking any easier.

She wondered how long they would be able to

keep up this pace, and she wondered about Buster as well. He still seemed enthusiastic about his job, but he was showing signs of slowing down. She ran her fingers through his coarse fur. He looked back at her almost as if he knew what she was thinking, then stood up from where he had been lying next to her.

The rest of the group took that as a cue and started to stand up and gather their bags and guns.

"Well, shall we?" Vince flung his bag over his shoulder.

Reese opened the bag containing the piece of scented material and let Buster reacquaint himself with it. Before she had time to close the bag and tuck it away, he was off and leading them down the road once more. She scrambled to shoulder her bag and follow as the others did the same. A few sighs and grunts from behind indicated that everyone was struggling as much as she was.

· 6 ·

Losing radio contact and the ability to communicate with the others at the motel weighed heavily on Vince's mind. He could tell it bothered John as well by the look of disappointment on his face when the radio check had failed. They were truly on their own out here, and the plan seemed to make less sense with every monotonous step forward.

Was it really a good idea to go after Ryan? Maybe they should have thought this through a little more. Although Vince couldn't think of a better plan of action right now, he started doubting this one and began to find flaws in it. That fact that he was tired, hot, and generally miserable didn't help matters any.

Last time they stopped to rest, Vince had considered the idea of sending Cy to retrieve a vehicle and then at least drive back this far. That way, they would have a car for their return trip.

His biggest hang-up was sending Cy back alone and, once again, the inability to communicate with anyone. Vince decided it was best to stick together and see this through. The trek back with Ryan would be difficult. For better or worse, though, they were committed to the plan now, and Vince couldn't help but think that with every step in this direction, they were a step farther from the motel and the relative safety of town.

When he and the others arrived at the looters' camp or wherever they were staying, with any luck they would be drunk and sleeping it off. Hopefully it wasn't too much farther. The plan wouldn't work if they couldn't make it back to the motel with Ryan by morning. Once the looters woke up and realized he was gone, the gig would be up and they would certainly launch an all-out attack on Cloverdale.

He was really hoping to have communication with the motel and have the option of calling for help and maybe a ride back, if it came to that. He still had the flare, but that was the last resort. Not only would it give away their position, but it would also force whoever came from the motel to attempt a blind rescue.

Without the radios, they wouldn't be able to let the others know what they were heading into or what they were up against. And even with the flare, a rescue attempt from the motel would be difficult. It wasn't like the flare would tell the others exactly where they were, just that they needed help.

Vince shook his head as he began to poke more and more holes in their plan to rescue Ryan. They were all tired, and maybe they had reacted too hastily to the kidnapping. More than anything, Tom's and Beverly's emotions had steered this course of action, but it wasn't like they had a choice in the matter. They all knew that handing over their supplies to the looters wasn't a viable option.

As Vince wrestled with his thoughts, he nearly walked into Reese, who was in front of him and had stopped dead in her tracks. Vince could tell something was wrong by her body language alone.

"What is it?" he asked.

"Buster hears something. Look." She pointed. Vince angled his headlamp to see down the road a ways and spotted Buster standing still on the shoulder of the road. The dog wasn't sniffing at the ground anymore. Instead, he was focused on some unseen point in the distance. Then they all heard a car approaching.

"Car!" John whispered the warning as loudly as he dared. "Get off the road now."

"Headlamps off!" Vince added.

"Buster, come here! Buster, here now!" Reese called out. Buster looked back at her and paused before letting out a low growl, then reluctantly scurried back to the group, periodically checking over his shoulder as he obeyed her command. The rest of them scattered like ants. Everyone but Tom ran to the right-hand shoulder and continued into the undergrowth.

When Vince realized that Tom had run to the opposite side of the road, it was too late to call him over to join them. The approaching vehicle was already too close and starting to illuminate the road beyond the next turn. It was too risky to have him change his position. Of all people in the group, Tom was not the one Vince wanted on his own right now.

Tom was consumed with hatred for the looters and wasn't thinking clearly. Vince was afraid that his emotions would get the best of him and that he would act out, but without any way to talk to him, they had to hope for the best. With any luck, Tom would keep his cool. Vince and John traded glances and shared a look of concern.

"Great, I hope he can keep it together," John said.

"Why did he go that way?" Cy asked. Reese had a tight grip on Buster's collar and had coaxed him into lying down beside her. Now they were all on their stomachs behind a thicket of musk thistle, an invasive species of plant that Vince had struggled to eradicate from his property for years. The spiny leaves made it difficult to handle without gloves and even more uncomfortable to hide in, but Vince was grateful for the cover it provided at the moment.

As the car approached, Vince was temporarily blinded by the headlights, and in an attempt to save his night vision, he closed his eyes as the beam of light crossed over their position. When he reopened them, he realized how slow the car was going and could see that it was an old Lincoln Continental. Vince had to remind himself to breathe as he watched the car, hoping it would continue on its way without incident. But to his horror, it came to an abrupt stop in the middle of the road, right where they had been standing moments ago.

Vince heard the rev of the engine shift to idle and saw the red glow of the brake lights diminish. He glanced down the line at John, Cy, and Reese and held his hand out to indicate that they should all remain still and not take any action. They nodded in agreement, and Vince turned his attention back to the car as the driver's door swung open with a loud metallic groan.

A man in a baseball hat stepped out of the car and stood there for a moment, looking around in every direction. He was searching for something, but what? Why had they stopped here of all places? Vince's heart began to race as he wondered if the man had seen them running for cover. But Vince and the others were well off the road by the time they came around the corner, so there was no way they were spotted.

The man left the door open and walked around it, making his way to the front of the car. He bent over to pick something up off the road.

"What is it?" a voice from inside the car called out. The man in the hat didn't answer and instead held up the item for his passenger to see. Vince couldn't tell what it was, but at least he knew the reason they had stopped. At first, he was relieved to know the car hadn't stopped because they had been spotted. But that feeling passed when the man in the hat turned to face the headlights and Vince saw what he was holding.

The man had one of the AR-15 magazines that John had given Tom. The passenger swung his door open and got out slowly; he was drinking a bottle of something. He tilted the bottle back and drained the last of its contents before he acknowledged the man in the hat again.

"I can't tell what that is." His speech was slurred.

"It's a full magazine, idiot," the man in the hat barked.

"So what? I gotta take a leak while we're stopped anyway." The passenger showed no interest in what his friend had found and turned to throw the bottle into the woods. Vince heard it land with a dull thud in the trees behind them. The passenger made his way to the back of the car, and then he staggered over to the shoulder on the opposite side of the road, where he proceeded to relieve himself. In the dim glow of the taillights, Vince saw a holstered pistol on the man's belt.

"Well, don't you think that's a little strange?" the man in the hat called out, clearly irritated with his inebriated passenger's attitude.

"So somebody dropped a mag. Big deal. Probably one of us." The passenger swayed as he finished up and adjusted his pants.

"Then why does it have 'Cloverdale Sheriff's Department' written on it?" the driver hollered back. Vince slid his shotgun close to his side as he glanced at John, who was way ahead of him.

"This is going downhill fast," John whispered. There was no way this was going to end well.

· 7 ·

"Sheriff's Department? That doesn't even make sense. Why would that be out here?" The passenger was suddenly interested and started to make his way back toward the car. The driver didn't answer him and instead tucked the magazine into his back pocket and drew a pistol from his belt. He began to scan the woods along both sides of the car.

The passenger rushed to join him but stumbled in the tall weeds along the shoulder and nearly fell into the bushes on the other side of the road.

"Whoa! Hey, what the... There's somebody over—" *Pop! Pop!* Vince could see the flicker of light from the other side of the car as Tom's AR rang out. The driver leveled his gun in Tom's direction and fired blindly into the woods. Vince rushed to pull his gun up and get in position to take a shot, but John beat him to the punch and squeezed off two rounds from his Glock.

The driver doubled over and dropped his gun.

He grasped at his stomach before falling to his knees in front of the car's headlights, where he remained a few seconds more. Then he fell to the ground in a writhing ball. Vince could hear his moans as he squirmed in agony.

Vince hopped up as fast as he could, ignoring his aching back. "Come on. We have to move fast."

"If the rest of their gang is anywhere near here, they probably heard that," John huffed as he stood, careful to keep his Glock trained on the driver.

"I'll check the other guy," Vince offered. He lowered his shotgun to his waist and slowly crept around the back end of the car. "Stay behind me, guys." Vince glanced back at Cy and Reese, then rounded the corner and looked for any signs of life.

The passenger was motionless and lying flat in the grass. Vince flicked on his headlamp with his left hand and held the shotgun on the body, finger on the trigger. He noticed two exit wounds in the man's upper torso and didn't see him breathing.

"Cy, grab the gun!"

Cy quickly slid the gun out of the holster and retreated to where Reese was crouched down and holding Buster's collar. Vince rolled the body over with his foot and satisfied himself that the man was in fact dead.

"Tom? Tom, where are you? Are you all right?" But there was no answer. Instead, Vince heard a feeble grunt from the bushes. Moments later, Tom staggered out, his left side completely covered in blood. Reese and Cy rushed over and helped him remain upright. Cy grabbed his gun while Reese provided support and helped him up to the edge of the road, where he sat down and leaned against the car.

Tom tilted his head back and clenched his teeth in pain. "My arm." He exhaled loudly.

Before Vince or Cy could react, Reese had Tom's shirt sleeve torn off and was rummaging through her backpack. After a few seconds, she pulled out a first aid kit and a bottle of water and began cleaning the blood from Tom's arm. With no way to help Reese, Vince was anxious to get some answers from the driver, if he was still alive.

"You got this under control?" Vince asked.

"Yep." Reese nodded but didn't look away from Tom.

"Hang in there, buddy. You're gonna be all right," Vince said as he headed for the front of the car. From what he could see, the wound looked pretty bad, but he wasn't about to admit it out loud.

When he reached John at the front of the car, he noticed the pistol the man was carrying had been kicked out of reach, and John was crouched down near the body.

"Where are they keeping the boy?" John spoke sternly, but the man didn't answer. Rather, he moved his head from side to side while wheezing and coughing up small amounts of blood. Vince couldn't determine if the man was refusing to give information or if he was actually struggling to talk.

The .45-caliber rounds from John's Glock hit the man in the gut and the thigh of his right leg. His clothes were thoroughly soaked in blood. John grabbed the man's face and forced him to remain still, smearing the blood that trickled from the corner of his mouth.

"Tell me where the boy is, and we'll get you help." John pushed him for information once more, but the man remained silent and looked away, trying to avoid eye contact with either of them.

John wiped his hand on the man's shirt. "It's no use. He's not going to talk."

"He knows where Ryan is. I know he does." Vince looked the driver over and saw that he was growing paler with each passing second. Judging by the size of the pool of blood that he was lying in, the guy wasn't long for this world. If they were going to get anything useful out of him, they would need to do it soon.

Vince grabbed the man's leg near the gunshot wound and squeezed hard. This caused the driver to half sit up before he fell back to the ground, wincing as he sucked in air loudly through clenched teeth.

"Aaah, p... Please stop. It hurts." The man groaned and tried to pull his leg away, but Vince held firm.

"The boy?" Vince insisted.

"Across from Put... Putnam Park, the racetrack off 550." The man's eyes rolled back into his head as he clawed at Vince's hand and tried to pry it off his leg. Vince pushed his hand away and continued to apply a fair amount of pressure to the wound.

"Where are they keeping him? Tell me now," Vince demanded.

"Ye... Yellow house. Barn out back." Vince released his leg, and the man let out a heavy sigh followed by another coughing fit that turned into a gurgling sound. Blood-colored bubbles spilled from his mouth.

"How many are there?" John pushed for more answers, but it was too late. The man had lost too much blood, and his body went limp as he turned his head and exhaled his last breath.

"He's gone." Vince wiped his hand on the man's pants before standing up and taking a step back.

"We need to get these bodies off the road and hidden in the woods before anyone else comes along." John stood up and looked at the passenger, who still lay where Tom had shot him. Vince grabbed the driver's legs while John retrieved the AR-15 magazine from his back pocket. Then they carried him to the edge of the road and heaved his body as far as they could on the count of three. When they returned to the car, they paused to check in on Tom.

Reese was still busy but making progress. She had already cinched Buster's collar above the wound to form a tourniquet and was putting the finishing touches on the gauze and tape around Tom's arm.

"How're you feeling?" Vince asked.

"Been better." Tom flashed an unconvincing smile as he looked away from his wound for a moment.

"He'll be okay. I gave him something for the pain, but we need to get him back to the motel so I can clean it out properly. The bullet is still in there, and it's hard to see what I'm doing out here." Reese's hands trembled slightly and were covered in blood. Vince could see that she was flustered, and she had every right to be. All things considered, she was doing great, and he was impressed with how she had jumped right in and went to work without hesitation.

"We can't go back without Ryan." Tom forced himself to sit up straight against the side of the car. They all looked at each other, but nobody said anything. Vince didn't want to risk losing Tom or, at best, making his injury worse. There was no hospital to take him to if his condition deteriorated. And while Reese had done an outstanding job field-dressing the wound, he knew she was at the limits of her skill and know-how with this type of injury. The poor girl was an aspiring veterinarian, and they were already asking too much of her. Plus, if something happened to Tom, Vince was sure she would take it to heart.

On the other hand, Vince didn't think a single one of them could talk Tom out of continuing with the rescue. At least they had a car and a destination now. Ultimately, it was up to Tom, and they already had their answer on that.

Cy and Reese helped Tom to his feet. "Come on. Let's finish this," Tom insisted. They all looked at each other again, but no one objected.

John was the first to speak up. "All right, then. Let's get this show on the road."

While John and Vince moved the other body off the shoulder and into the woods, Reese and Cy helped situate Tom in the back seat. Cy gathered both pistols the looters had been carrying and joined Reese and Buster in the back as well. Vince knew where they needed to go, so John let him drive this time.

When Vince climbed into the still-running Lincoln, the first thing he noticed was the mess. There were empty beer cans scattered around the floor, and as much as he hated to do it, he threw them out onto the road. The last thing he wanted was a can rolling under one of the pedals.

"Nasty people," John snarled as he emptied his side as well.

"That's nothing. You should see the back," Reese remarked.

Vince finished clearing out his side and closed the door. Pausing for a moment, he looked back at Reese. "Thanks for what you did back there. I'm really proud of the way you handled that."

"Yeah, thanks." Tom gingerly placed his right hand over the bandage.

She shrugged. "No problem. Cy helped, too."

"Not much. That was all you. I just handed you stuff," he added.

"You both did a great job." Vince nodded at Cy as he looked at them all crammed in the back seat. Thankfully, it was a big car, but three people and an eighty-pound dog were pushing it, even for an old Lincoln Continental.

"Come on, boy. Come on." Vince smacked the front seat with his hand a couple of times. It didn't take much convincing for Buster to accept the offer and launch himself into the front seat between him and John. Vince did a quick three-point turn and headed for the Putnam Park racetrack.

· 8 ·

The Putnam Park road course was a small amateur racetrack used by local auto enthusiast clubs. Vince had been there many times to watch the weekend races, and on occasion, he filled in as part of the pit crew for a few of his friends.

The track was pretty far out in the middle of nowhere and about a thirty-minute drive from Cloverdale. While he didn't know exactly where the looters were keeping Ryan, it couldn't be that hard to find a yellow house with a barn nearby. As he recalled, there were only a few houses close to the track on County Road 550, so he was fairly confident they could figure it out.

Tom apologized a few times for dropping the magazine and causing the looters to stop, but they were lucky, really. Sure, it could have gone badly, but it didn't. And making this trip on foot would have taken them well past sunrise and ruined any chance they had of surprising the looters at night.

Vince drove cautiously and only used the headlights when absolutely necessary. Navigating with the running lights and the little bit of moonlight they had made for slow going, but it was worth it, and John agreed. There was no telling when or if they'd run into more of the gang, but now was no time to be careless. This road was the most direct way to Cloverdale from the track and was undoubtedly the route the looters were using, as evidenced by the occasional beer can or bottle on the road.

They finally made the turn onto South County Road 550. It was only a half mile or so until they reached the racetrack. This area was largely agricultural, and the wheat fields here had been cut already, leaving short stubble behind and a clear view of the farmhouses between them and the Putnam Park road course. Vince shut all the lights off and pulled onto the shoulder as John used his binoculars to scan the surrounding farms for any signs of life.

"I don't see anything." John passed the binoculars to Vince, who took a turn looking for any sign of activity.

"No, me neither." Vince checked his watch. "It's pushing 3:00, though. I imagine they're all passed out by now."

"They'll probably have somebody on watch, like we do at the motel. Don't you think?" Tom leaned forward in the seat and seemed to have found a renewed sense of vigor.

"We should go the rest of the way on foot." Vince reached up and turned the dome light off so it wouldn't give them away when the doors opened. He shut the car down and left the keys in the ignition as he climbed out. Buster was right behind him and immediately found a place to take a leak. Everyone else got out of the car and gathered on the shoulder, looking across the fields and toward the farms.

"It's got to be one of those three farms, but I can't tell for the life of me which one has a yellow house." John used the binoculars again to look across the vast open area in front of them. These were the only farms on the road, and they were directly across from the track. Provided the driver was telling the truth, Ryan was being held at one of those properties.

"Tom, why don't you stay behind and be the wheelman. We may need to get out of there in a hurry." Vince wasn't crazy about the idea of Tom driving with one arm, but it might be the only way to convince him to stay back while the others went after Ryan.

"Not a chance. I still got one good arm and my trigger finger works just fine. Besides, you're going to need all the eyes and ears you can get out there." Vince knew that it was pointless to argue with the man and decided to save his energy.

"Reese and Cy, you guys stay here with Buster in the car and be ready. Reese, you and Buster have done enough for one night. Cy, I need you behind the wheel. I trust your driving as much as I trust myself." Vince hoped it was a good enough sales pitch to keep them both out of harm's way.

"Dad, I can help," Cy protested.

"You are helping: by staying here. Please, I need you to do this."

"Fine, but if you get into trouble, we'll be there in no time."

While Vince was trying to convince Cy to stay put, John made one last attempt to contact Bill on the radio. As Vince suspected, there was no answer.

John gave up after another couple of tries and tossed the radio back into the car. "No point in carrying dead weight."

Reese called Buster back in from one of the nearby fields, where he was making his way toward an irrigation ditch. Vince and the other two men did a quick gear check and made sure their guns were loaded and ready. They were leaving their backpacks and traveling as light as they could. The plan was to sneak in unnoticed, grab Ryan, and get out just the same. They were about ready to start across the field when Vince turned back toward the car.

"If you see headlights coming your way, I want

you to backtrack on this road carefully and cut over to the next county road to the east. We'll meet you there if we can't get back to this location. Understand?"

"Got it," Cy said bluntly. He sounded less than enthusiastic about his new role, but without any guilt whatsoever, Vince was willing to accept a sour attitude over risking his son's life. He hated to treat him like this, but they really did need a wheelman and he really did trust Cy's ability to drive. He just hoped his son understood that.

The first of the small farms was less than half a mile from their location, but they had to cross an open field to get there. Even though it was plenty dark out, the air was a lot cleaner out here, and when the clouds parted, the almost-full moon did a decent job of lighting up the night. If the looters had someone on lookout, silhouettes walking across the field would be easy to spot. Vince didn't know if the gang would be disciplined enough to have someone on watch, but he wasn't willing to gamble their lives on it.

They used a series of irrigation ditches that ran through the fields in a grid pattern to approach the farms. It would take longer to travel along the ditches, but they provided the best cover thanks to the occasional tree growing along the edges and the continuous band of overgrown weeds that lined the banks.

Vince, John, and Tom set out for the first ditch. The wheat stubble crunching underfoot sounded ridiculously loud in the still of the night. Vince looked back at the car once more. Cy and Reese were in the front seat with Buster between them. Vince hated leaving them there, but it was the better option, although there was no guarantee that another car with looters wouldn't be out and patrolling the roads. But that was a chance they would have to take.

Hopefully they could locate Ryan and be out of here in a short amount of time. The sooner they could return to Cloverdale, the better. Once the looters realized they had lost their bargaining chip, there was no doubt they would retaliate with everything they had, so Vince and the others needed to prepare for the ensuing attack. He tried to put the thought out of his mind. First things first: right now, they needed to rescue Ryan.

. 9 .

The first irrigation ditch they came to was only four or five feet wide and a couple of feet deep. It had a large number of healthy weeds growing along its banks, some as tall as a few feet. Between the height of the weeds and the depth of the ditch, they would be completely concealed. Vince wasn't looking forward to getting wet, but it was the price they would have to pay for a stealthy approach.

Without hesitation, Vince led the way and jumped down into the shallow trench. He expected to land in stagnant water and smelly mud, but there was none. To his surprise, he found himself standing on firm, dry ground. This time of year, the ditches should be full of water and teeming with frogs from the spring rains. He knew this because the early summer irrigation ditches around his family farm provided hours of entertainment and frog catching when he was a boy.

He thought there was something missing when they were standing around the car, but he couldn't put his finger on it. The night was dead silent, and it made sense now; there simply wasn't enough water to sustain life. The unseasonably high temperatures and lack of rain had left the ditches dry, and the flourishing weeds had sucked up whatever moisture remained.

Vince flipped his headlamp on for a second. Careful to shield it with his hand, he focused the dim red light on the ground. There at his feet he saw the cracked and dry ground that had once been mud. It was a sad realization and another reminder that things were very different now.

There was an upside, however, to the dry and barren waterway: the ability to move in near silence. The hard-packed dirt lacked any vegetation, providing a clear, easy-to-navigate path all the way to their destination.

They were able to move quickly and quietly through the empty ditch and arrived at the first farm in a matter of minutes. But as they closed in on the property, Vince realized that the place had burned down like so many other homes. This clearly wasn't the looters' place, so they moved on. Still able to use the irrigation ditch, they made their way to the next farm.

They had to pass through a small stand of hardwoods and bushes to get a good look at the next place, and once they cleared the trees, they knew they had found the looters. There was an assortment of four-wheelers, motorcycles, cars, and trucks parked around the property. The farm itself consisted of two houses and a barn. The older home sat near the front of the property and was completely dark. Only a half dozen vehicles were parked there.

The house nearest to them was much newer and larger. Moonlight reflected off the solar panels on the roof, more proof that solar electric systems had saved the homes and businesses that remained. A faint light also emanated from a small porch on the back side of the house. The barn was located a couple hundred yards from the house and was at the back of the property. It was the closest building to Vince and his group and not too far from the tree line.

There was no activity, but Vince didn't expect any at this hour of the morning. From where he was, he couldn't see the front of the barn, and no windows on the back or the side were visible from the woods.

"All right. We're going to have to do this quietly. Shooting is our last resort," Vince whispered and looked at Tom to make sure he was paying attention.

"If Ryan's in the barn, I'm sure they've got somebody watching him. Maybe more around the main house," John whispered back.

"Nice and easy. Let's go." Vince led the way and crept toward the barn, doing his best to keep a low profile. With Tom bringing up the rear, they approached in a single-file line until they reached the back corner of the building. They paused there for a minute and listened while they peered around the side of the barn and scanned their surroundings. John scurried to the opposite corner and took a peek before returning and reporting that he had seen nothing from there, either.

At this distance, Vince could tell the light they saw from the woods was a small yellowish-colored porch light. Had it most likely been left on by mistake? There was nobody on the porch, and if there was a man on guard, he was nowhere to be seen or he was off making his rounds; the thought of that was concerning, but they had to keep moving.

They crept along the far side of the barn, which wasn't visible from the house, until they reached the front corner. Vince very carefully peeked around. The barn was typical and had a large rolling door on the front side and a smaller man door next to it. The large door was cracked open a few feet, and a dim sliver of light spilled out onto the gravel driveway. Vince could hear voices coming from inside. He leaned back around the corner and faced the others.

"I hear a couple people in the barn," Vince whispered. "I'm gonna take a look." He gently leaned his shotgun against the building. He didn't want to attempt this while holding the large weapon and wasn't planning on making a move yet; he just wanted to do a little recon and see what they were dealing with. He had his .45 on him if things went south.

He went low to the ground and crawled on all fours to the smaller man door. The upper half of the door was glass, and as he straightened up on two knees, he could see inside the barn. Two men sat on bales of hay and were using another bale between them as a card table. The lantern hanging off a support post above them wasn't very bright, but it produced enough light for Vince to see the two rifles leaning on the post beneath it and a partially empty bottle of whiskey on the ground. He leaned left and right, trying to get a better angle and see more of the interior layout of the barn, but he still couldn't locate Ryan. He was going to have to move in a little closer and take a look from the partially open door.

Vince went prone again, this time on his hands and knees, and crawled to the corner of the main barn door. From here, he could see the rest of the interior and spotted Ryan immediately. The poor kid had a handcuff around one of his ankles. The other end was attached to a chain that was wrapped around another support column. A padlock held it all together.

Ryan was sitting on the floor with his back to the post, arms wrapped around his knees tightly and his face hidden from sight. Vince couldn't tell if he was sleeping or not, but with the two men playing cards and talking loudly, he doubted it.

Vince felt his blood pressure rising as he tried to push down the feelings of anger and hatred for these people. What kind of animals would keep a kid Ryan's age—or anyone for that matter—chained up in a barn? Suddenly, one of the men stood up and stretched. He mumbled something about taking care of business. He grabbed his rifle and slung it over his shoulder. After taking a quick shot from the bottle, he headed toward the door and straight toward Vince.

Vince yanked his head back from the doorway and shot up to his feet. Then he hurried back to the corner of the building, careful to duck below the half glass door on his way.

"Back, back, back," Vince whispered, motioning with his hands for John and Tom to retreat to the back corner of the building. They reacted quickly, retreated to their original hiding spot, and were hidden in a matter of seconds.

"Do they have Ryan?" Tom asked before Vince could say anything.

"Yes, and there's two guys watching him. One of them is coming out to go to the bathroom, I think." Vince leaned around the corner just in time to see the man walking toward the woods, whistling as he went. Now was their chance to do something.

· 10 ·

As the man continued out to the edge of the woods, Vince turned and quickly laid out his plan to John and Tom.

Vince would take the whistler out while the other two moved up to the corner of the barn closest to the door. After Vince had dealt with his guy, he would do his best to impersonate him and call the other man out. Hopefully, the remaining guard wouldn't be able to see well enough to tell the difference between Vince and his friend. Once he was within reach, John and Tom could take care of him.

The man continued to whistle to himself as he made his way over to an old horse trailer parked at the edge of the woods. Considering what disgusting slobs they were, Vince was surprised that he had walked so far to relieve himself, but he was glad he did. The whistling helped mask any noise Vince made during his approach, and as he crept up behind him, the man was blissfully unaware of what was about to happen.

Vince covered the last couple of feet swiftly and placed a hand over the man's mouth while bringing his right arm around the neck. Then he squeezed with all his strength. The man struggled and flailed his arms, but it was in vain and only made Vince more determined to hang on and finish the job quickly. He stopped trying to grab Vince and reached for some imaginary salvation out in front of him. A few seconds later, the man's arms dropped to his side and went limp. Vince was about to lower the guy to the ground, but something came over him and he hung on. He continued to apply pressure for a while longer until he felt the legs give out. Only then did he relax his grip, step backward, and lower the body to the ground.

He grabbed the rifle and leaned it against the trailer while he searched the man's pockets for the key to Ryan's handcuffs or the padlock. All he found was a pack of cigarettes, a lighter, and a pocket knife. Vince gave up his search and dragged the body several feet into the woods until it was out of sight.

When he was done hiding the guard's body, he took the rifle and slung it over his shoulder. Looking back, he made sure that John and Tom were in position. He could barely make them out, even though they were no more than twenty yards away. He could see their dark figures crouched at the corner of the barn, and he knew it was time to draw the other guard outside.

"Hey, come look at this!" Vince called out to the other guard as loud as he dared without risking someone hearing him from the house. He waited, but there was no reply. Then he tried a low-pitched whistle. A few seconds later, he saw a head pop out from the doorway.

"What?" an irritated voice asked.

Vince motioned with his hand for the man to come to him. It worked, and the man started walking toward Vince.

"What is it, man?" He sounded more irritated this time, and as he passed the corner of the barn, he didn't notice the two men waiting for him.

"Hey!" John whispered. The guard was startled by the voice and spun around to meet the butt end of an AR-15 face-first. The crack of the gun against his face made Vince flinch a little. The body fell to the ground with a heavy thud.

Vince jogged over to where John and Tom were standing, and they all stared at the man for a second—only it wasn't a man at all. Now that they were close, Vince could see that he was no more than a kid who couldn't have been more than sixteen or seventeen years old. His nose was badly broken, and his face and shirt were covered in blood.

Vince looked to see if the kid was still breathing, but he didn't see any movement. John was visibly shocked and clearly wasn't expecting his target to be so young.

Vince tried to move things along. "Check his pockets for a key."

John rummaged through his pockets, occasionally glancing at the kid's face. "Nothing."

"I'll deal with this. Go get Ryan." Vince barely had the words out of his mouth before Tom was off and into the barn with John right behind him. If they couldn't find the key, John would be the one who could get the cuffs off Ryan. Meanwhile, Vince wanted to hide this body as well. If they made it out of here tonight without being seen, it might buy them some time.

When the looters discovered that Ryan was gone, they would know what happened immediately. But if the two guards were missing as well, maybe the rest of the looters would think they had taken Ryan for themselves and tried to work out their own deal for the supplies. It was worth a try and the few extra minutes it took Vince to drag the body into the woods.

By the time Vince returned, John and Tom were coming out of the barn with Ryan. John was carrying their rifles and Tom was carrying Ryan with his good arm.

"Found the key inside." John had his hands full

with three rifles, and Vince had his shotgun and the other guard's gun. It would be helpful if Ryan could travel on his own, but Vince didn't have the heart to ask Tom to put his son down and carry his weapon just yet.

"How is he?" Vince asked.

"Fine, I think. Just scared and tired," Tom answered.

"Can you sling one of these rifles over your bad arm?" John held out one of the newly acquired weapons, a wooden-stocked hunting rifle with a leather sling.

"Yeah, I guess so." Tom took the gun and gently slid it over his left shoulder with John's help.

"All right, you guys, get a head start," John said. "I'll be right behind you. I just need a couple minutes." He turned to look at the house.

"What are you talking about?" Vince asked. "We're all leaving together, now." For the first time, Ryan lifted his head from his dad's shoulder, and Vince could see that he had been crying.

"We might not get another chance like this. I want to try and disable some of their vehicles, even if it's temporary, like slashing their tires."

"What if someone hears you or they have someone on lookout and you get caught?" Tom asked.

"It's a chance I'm willing to take. If we do this right, it could buy us a few days of peace and quiet.

It would give us a chance to get on our feet. Besides, I'm pretty sure the other guy in the barn was supposed to be on lookout. You don't assign two guys to watch a child in handcuffs." John leaned the ARs against the back side of the barn.

He clearly intended on doing this with or without Vince and Tom's blessing. As appealing as it was to make a clean getaway right then and there, Vince had to admit that sabotaging the vehicles was a good idea. It made a lot of sense and wouldn't necessarily ruin his plan. The other looters might think the two men on watch had done it. John also made a good point about one of the guards most likely being the house lookout.

"I'm in." Vince leaned his two weapons next to John's.

"You don't have to do this, Vince. I can handle it," John offered.

"No way I'm letting you have all the fun."

John nodded. "All right, then. Tom, we'll see you at the car in a little bit."

"Be careful, guys." Tom paused long enough to look them both in the eyes before turning and heading off toward the woods and into the shadows with Ryan.

Vince checked his watch. It was close to four in the morning, and the thought crossed his mind that the looters might be changing out guard duty, but he had no way of knowing for sure.

"Hopefully neither one of these guys is getting relieved anytime soon," Vince said.

"Yeah, I thought about that, too. We'll just have to be quick."

They made their way off the gravel lane that led to the barn and traveled over the grass to minimize the noise they made. They went as fast as they could while keeping an eye out for any movement in and around the house. John pulled out his pocket knife when they reached the first car.

"Let's split up. We'll get this done a lot quicker." Without warning, John sank his knife into the rear tire of the car. It let out a loud hiss as Vince peered over the hood and watched the house. He hated how much noise it made and was worried that someone would eventually hear them if they kept it up. John's idea was well-intentioned but too noisy. Vince had something much more sinister in mind, not to mention quieter.

"I think that's going to get their attention. Let's go for the brakes." Vince would have liked to do more damage to the vehicles rather than just tamper with the brakes, but there was no way they'd be able to get under the hoods without waking up someone in the house. Taking out the brakes was a good alternative.

The looters would notice the deflated tires right away, and if any of them were handy, they could eventually fix them and resume their nefarious activities. But the lack of brakes could cause some serious trouble and, with any luck, some major accidents—maybe even permanently take out some of these vehicles, along with whoever was unfortunate enough to be driving. Anything they could do to even the odds would be worth the effort, and thanks to what the looters had already done to Vince and the others, he could do what was needed without having a guilty conscience.

· 11 ·

"Keep an eye out for me." Vince lay on his back and shimmied under the car they were hiding behind.

John looked under the car at him. "What are you doing?"

"Brakes," Vince replied as he found the brake lines and grabbed hold of the thin metal tubing. He worked it back and forth until there was a substantial split between the tube and the fitting. He checked the damage out with his headlamp and made sure the brake fluid was leaking out at a good pace.

Vince wished he could break the lines off completely, but it was too much work. If they wanted to disable all the vehicles parked here, there wasn't enough time—not to mention that he really didn't want to get covered in brake fluid. Besides, it might work out for the best if the lines bled slowly. When the looters took the cars out, they would finish the job themselves by applying pressure to the brakes and blowing the rest of the fluid out. Hopefully they would do this while driving at a decent speed.

Even if the looters figured out that the vehicles had been tampered with and didn't have any accidents, the brake lines would be hard to fix. There might be a decent mechanic who could patch the lines, but without total replacement, they would never be as good as new. With handicapped vehicles, the looters would be at a serious disadvantage.

At the very least, doing this would buy them time, like John said, and that was something that Vince and the others desperately needed if they were ever going to accomplish anything back in town. Even a couple of days without having to worry about the looters would be huge. It would give them time to build up their defenses and complete some of the bigger tasks—or at least get them well underway.

Vince and John made their way from one vehicle to the next, careful to keep a watchful eye on the house as they moved. Vince was at a loss with the ATVs and motorcycles, and other than removing the spark plug wires, he wasn't sure how to cause the most damage. It would have been nice to have Cy there with them. He would have known exactly how to do some type of permanent damage.

Instead, Vince guessed and randomly pulled at any exposed wires or tubing, hoping for the best.

He glanced at his watch and saw that they had been at it for nearly thirty minutes. Cy and the others back at the car were probably starting to worry, so they needed to wrap it up and head back soon. Only one pickup truck remained, and as they made their way over to it, a light came on inside the house.

"Hey!" John whispered.

"I see it." Vince and John crouched behind the pickup. Determined to finish what they had started, Vince wasted no time shimmying under the old Chevy and locating the brake lines. It didn't take long, and Vince was able to work quickly. There was more room under the pickup thanks to a lift kit and oversized tires.

He finished up and rolled out from under the truck just in time to hear a screen door slam. His heart raced as he looked at John, who was peering over the truck bed and staring intently at the house. John quickly crouched down and joined Vince on the ground. He put his finger to his lips and pointed toward the house, then put one finger in the air and mouthed the word "one."

Vince smelled cigarette smoke almost instantly, and he hoped the guy had just stepped outside for a quick smoke and would head back in soon. He glanced at his watch impatiently; this was costing them time. They had already been here too long, and it probably felt much longer to Cy and the others waiting at the car.

"Where is he?" they heard the man on the porch say to himself. No doubt he was looking for one of the men he and John had taken out. This guy was probably supposed to take over for one of them, which meant he wasn't going back inside after his smoke.

"I swear, can't trust nobody to do their job," the man huffed. Vince heard his heavy footsteps on the wooden porch steps. He was coming their way. If only they'd have worked a little faster, they could have avoided this guy. Vince was mad at himself for taking the extra time and waiting to make sure the brake lines on every vehicle were actually leaking fluid.

The truck he and John were hiding behind was less than ten yards from the house and parked a couple of feet from the dirt lane that led back to the barn. A few seconds later, they heard the crunch of gravel as the man made his way down the driveway and toward the barn.

Vince looked under the truck, trying to see where the man was, but he couldn't see well enough to locate him. He could only hear the approaching footsteps.

John leaned in close to Vince. "I got this," he whispered. John crept to the end of the truck and waited for the man to pass by. A moment later the footsteps turned into a dark figure that stood no more than three feet away from the back of the truck. The man was walking slowly, and Vince could see the glowing end of his cigarette as he passed. John stood up quietly, pulled out his Glock, and took a couple of steps toward the man.

For a brief moment, Vince worried that John was going to shoot the man, but he realized the plan when John raised his hand with the gun in it. John brought the handle of the gun down on the back of the man's neck with a sickening thud. The cigarette fell from his mouth and hit the ground as he turned to see what had hit him. But he only made it halfway around before his knees buckled and he joined his cigarette on the ground.

Vince shot up from his hiding spot and glanced back at the house. There were no signs of anyone else, but it stood to reason that another guard would come along soon to relieve the other guy who was watching Ryan. They needed to get out of here before that happened. Although the thought to wait there and take the next guy out as well crossed Vince's mind, it was too risky and Cy was probably beyond worried at this point. They had pushed their luck enough for one night. It was time to go.

Vince joined John on the driveway and helped him lift the guy over his shoulder. The man had a revolver in his waistband, and Vince took it and stuffed it into his belt. He was feeling pretty good about their mission right now. They had taken out five looters, including the two back on the road, picked up as many weapons, and handicapped most of their vehicles, at least the ones that were parked at the main house.

By the count of cars, trucks, ATVs, and motorcycles, they were dealing with a large gang—much larger than he had anticipated. If he had to guess, this was some type of motorcycle gang or something like that. There must have been thirty or more vehicles around the house, including motorcycles and ATVs. There were no gangs around here that Vince knew of, and he wondered where they had come from. They weren't local, at least not all of them.

Unfortunately, the house at the front of the property looked like it had a few vehicles parked around it as well, but it was too far away and too much of a risk to mess with. He and John debated it, but ultimately they decided to not push their luck. For all they knew, someone was most likely standing watch at that house, too.

Vince gathered the guns they had left at the barn while John took the body into the woods and hid it. He waited for John at the edge of the trees, where they had first entered the property. When John caught up to him, Vince handed him a couple of the rifles to carry.

"I guess they'll know it was us now," Vince said.

"What makes you say that?" John asked.

"When that guy comes to, he'll tell them what happened."

"That's not gonna be a problem." John turned and headed into the woods. Vince was surprised at John's response, but he didn't say anything further and followed his friend.

· 12 ·

Vince ran John's comment through his head a couple of times before he realized what he meant—or at least what he thought it meant. Had John finished the guy off? That was why John had taken a few extra minutes to catch up with him at the edge of the property?

Vince was going to ask him to clarify his statement but decided not to. He knew what he meant without asking, and it bothered him for some reason. Vince had killed more people in the last five days than he cared to think about, but somehow it felt different. Those were in the moment. He didn't think less of John for doing what had to be done, but it made him think about what they were becoming.

Were they any better than this gang of looters? Vince forced the thought from his mind. Of course they were. It was different. They were fighting for their lives. Vince and the others weren't the ones attacking and kidnapping people. He thought about poor Ryan handcuffed to the post in the barn and the look on the boy's face when he glanced up from his dad's shoulder. As they made their way through the woods and down into the first ditch, all doubt about what they were doing and how they were doing it vanished from his mind.

The looters had brought this upon themselves. They were the aggressors, and whatever Vince and the others had to do was justified. He pictured Bill lying in a pool of blood in the motel parking lot as Reese struggled to help him. He thought about all the times he and the others had been shot at in the last few days alone. He couldn't help but wonder if he would ever be able to trust anyone outside his small group again.

He hated who he was becoming and wondered if the others felt the same. But mostly he thought about how this would affect Cy, Reese, and the younger kids. Ryan would certainly never forget tonight. It would haunt his dreams for the rest of his life. Like it or not, this was their life now: running through ditches, trying to outsmart bad guys, and fighting for their lives.

It was still plenty dark out, but Vince recognized the last series of irrigation trenches they were in and looked up as he tried to locate the car.

"Hang on a second." Vince paused and set the guns down against his leg while he tried to catch his breath. He was smoked and just needed a minute to get his bearings. They had to be close now. John stopped as well and used the rifles he was carrying to prop himself up while he panted heavily. It was a good thing the air was cleaner out here in the country. Otherwise, they would have both been hacking up a lung by now. As it was, Vince's throat was burning like it had during the first couple of days after the bombs. He wished now they had brought some water with them.

Vince reached up and flashed the red light on his headlamp toward where he thought the car was. The last thing he wanted was for him and John to be mistaken for bad guys and risk any friendly fire. Cy and the others had no idea what was going on and were probably more than a little on edge right now. He was rewarded with a few faint red flashes off to his left and less than a couple of hundred yards away.

Knowing they were almost back at the car gave him a sense of relief and a slight boost of energy. He didn't have much left in him; this was the most exercise he'd seen in a while. His heart was pounding, and his legs were growing weaker by the second, but they were almost there.

They covered the last bit of distance to the car more slowly than when they had come out, but John was in the lead, and Vince wasn't about to complain.

"What took you guys so long?" Reese asked. "We were getting worried."

"We took out most of their vehicles and had to deal with another guy who came out of the house," John answered between breaths.

Tom and Ryan were in the back seat, and Ryan looked to be sleeping on his dad's lap.

"How's the arm?" Vince asked.

Tom nodded. "It hurts, but I'm fine. Glad you're back."

"Cy, can you pop the trunk?" Vince asked. "We've got a few new weapons to add to our collection." Cy met them at the back of the car and helped them unload their spoils into the Lincoln's massive trunk. Vince was eager to look them over and see exactly what they had acquired, but he was too tired and too anxious to return to the relative safety of the motel.

"Let's get out of here." Vince slammed the trunk and put his hand on Cy's shoulder. "You're driving."

Cy was surprised to hear his dad relinquish the driving responsibility to him, but it made sense. He'd never seen his dad look so tired before in his life. Soaked with sweat and moving slowly, both his dad and John looked bushed. But as much as he worried about them, there was no denying that they knew what they were doing and had accomplished what they had set out to do.

Cy was ashamed to admit it, but at the start of the rescue mission, he didn't think they would actually get Ryan back. It felt like they were looking for a needle in a haystack. Even with Buster tracking the scent, he was doubtful. Yet here they were: a little worse for wear but on their way back with Ryan—and a few extra weapons to boot.

Cy wished he could have gone along with them to the looters' place, but he understood why his dad wanted him to stay behind with the car. It was an important job, and as unpredictable as the looters were, it made sense to be ready in case another car came along. Of course, he also figured it was a way for his dad to keep him and Reese out of harm's way. Sooner or later, his dad would have to come to terms with the fact that he couldn't always protect him. But this wasn't the time or place to get into that.

What would have happened if Cy had listened to his dad when they were trapped behind the roadblock? He was trying to be patient and things from his father's perspective, but it was hard sometimes and often felt like he was being treated like he was still just a kid. His dad had always been a little overprotective, and given their current circumstances, that certainly wasn't going to change.

Nobody said a word as they made their way back to the motel. Vince, John, and Tom, with Ryan on his lap, were all in the back seat while Reese and Buster remained in the front with Cy. He glanced in the rearview mirror occasionally and checked on his dad. They all had their heads back on the seat and their eyes closed. It had been a long night on top of an already long day. Cy wondered if they would work on any of the projects tomorrow or if everyone would lay low after all this and rest. It was fine with him if they had a down day, but he knew his dad too well and doubted that would actually happen.

The other reason he kept checking the rearview mirror was that he half expected to see headlights any second now. His dad and John filled them in on what they had done to the looters' vehicles, but they didn't disable them all, and the thought of being chased bothered him. If he was sure of anything, it was that the looters were relentless and would seek revenge. His dad and John had dealt the looters a big blow tonight, but the fight was far from over.

· 13 ·

Vince jumped as he woke up, startled by the movement of the car as Cy swerved to avoid a wreck on the road. He must have dozed off for a minute or two. He rubbed at his eyes while struggling to find his bearings and figure out where exactly they were. Then he spotted the overpass up ahead and realized that they were almost back in Cloverdale.

He looked over at John, who was awake but looked like he was in a daze.

"Have you tried the radio?" Vince asked him.

"Yeah, I got a hold of Bill. He's making a way through the roadblock for us with the loader."

Vince looked at the others in the car. Ryan was still sleeping, and Tom didn't appear far behind. His arm looked bad, and now that Vince was close enough to see better, he noticed that Tom had lost more blood than he previously thought. Not only was his shirt soaked, but his pants were as well.

Vince thought about telling Cy to drive faster, but he didn't want to push their luck and risk crashing into something. Maybe he should have insisted that Tom stay behind at the car with Cy and Reese, but he doubted he would have listened; exerting himself by running through the ditches while carrying Ryan certainly hadn't helped his situation and was probably responsible for the further blood loss.

Within a matter of minutes, they were passing through the roadblock. Vince saw Bill behind the wheel of the loader, which had one of the roadblock cars on its forks. As soon as they passed, Bill went about replacing the car and closing off the entrance.

When Cy pulled into the motel parking lot, everyone was waiting out front and swarmed the car as it came to a stop. Beverly was first at the rear passenger door. She yanked it open and took Ryan from Tom's arms. The boy barely woke up and clung to Beverly as she helped her husband out of the car.

"Tom! Your arm. What happened?" She burst into tears.

"Calm down, calm down. I'll be all right. I just need to lie down." Tom tried his best to put her at ease, but it wasn't working.

"Don't lie down," Reese said. "Whatever you do. I need you sitting upright in a chair. I just want to grab a few things, and I'll be over. We need to get that bullet out now." She didn't waste any time and ran to her room to collect what she needed.

Fred and Mary took over for Beverly and helped Tom into his room. Reese was right behind them, carrying a basket loaded with stuff from the pharmacy.

"Want to help me out?" she called to Cy as she ran by with Buster chasing behind. "I'm going to need someone to hold a light."

"Coming," Cy answered.

As Vince and John stretched their legs, Bill parked the loader alongside the curb and shut it down.

"You think we'll see them anytime soon?" John looked toward the interstate.

Vince knew he was referring to the looters. "I sure hope not, but I wouldn't bet on it."

He didn't plan on taking any chances, either.

"Hey, Bill, can you hang in there and stay on watch for a while?" Vince asked as he approached them.

"I'm on till six anyway," he replied.

Vince and John gave Bill a quick rundown of their adventures as they sorted through the newly acquired weapons in the trunk. The pistols were a 9mm, a .45, and a .38 revolver. They were all fully loaded except for the .38, which was missing one round—the one in Tom's arm. Vince was glad to see that he had been shot by the smaller-caliber pistol and shuddered to think what the .45 or the 9mm would have done at that range.

They also picked up two new rifles: an open-sight 30-30 lever-action and a .22 rifle that was also open-sighted. None of the guns were that impressive, nor were they that well-maintained. Still, it was good to add to their stockpile and it was better than nothing, but there was no extra ammo for them, so in the end, they weren't really a big help.

There was nothing else of note in the car, mostly trash and empty beer cans, but Vince did find a bottle of whiskey under an old tire in the trunk.

"Maybe you ought to take that into Tom," John said. "I imagine he might need it."

"Yeah, it might help a little, but more as a token. I'm sure Reese will give him something for the pain. At least I hope." No sooner had Vince spoken the words than they heard a muffled yell from Tom's room.

John frowned. "Too late I guess."

Vince felt bad for the man, but there was nothing he could do to help. As it was, there were probably too many people standing around and watching Reese work. The poor girl was under enough pressure already, and she didn't need another pair of eyes watching over her shoulder.

John excused himself, and Vince watched as he

retreated quietly to his room and closed the door. He couldn't help but worry about his friend. The guard John had taken out back at the looters' farm was young, and the look on John's face when he realized how young spoke volumes. The kid was probably only a few years younger than John's son. The guy had been through enough already. As if losing his family wasn't enough, he would now have that on his conscience.

Vince wanted nothing more than to go to his and Mary's room and lie down, but he felt obligated to wait and at least find out if Reese had removed the bullet. Even though Tom had brought this on himself by dropping the magazine, Vince couldn't help but feel partly responsible for what happened. Everything had worked out for the best, but things could have gone very differently. Thinking about some of the other possible outcomes made him cringe.

He found a spot on the hood of the Lincoln and hoisted himself up. As he sat there, he thought about everything they had been through in the last twenty-four hours. It barely seemed possible, like not enough time had passed for everything to have happened. In his current state of exhaustion, the past day's events felt more like a bad dream than reality.

The bottle of whiskey was too much to resist, and he reasoned that he'd earned a shot at least. Besides, it might help ease the constant pain in his lower back. He was far too old to be running around the woods at night.

As it went down, the whiskey burned his throat, and he felt the warmth wash over him like a blanket. He took one more sip before putting the cap back on and setting the bottle down on the hood. He glanced back at Bill and thought about offering him some, but he decided against it. A few sips of whiskey would be just enough to make someone sleepy, and that wouldn't be much help when Bill was sitting alone in the truck while on watch.

Finally, the others started to emerge from Tom's room. One by one, they filed out. Fred paused and gave Vince a nod, indicating that everything had gone all right.

"I'll be out in a bit to relieve you," Fred called out to Bill. Vince checked his watch. It was after five in the morning, and the eastern horizon was beginning to show signs of a rising sun. Another hot day lay ahead, although he doubted much would get done. They all needed rest. Even those who had stayed behind probably hadn't slept much.

Reese was the last one out of the room. Cy held the door and closed it behind her. She was wiping blood off her hands with a wet rag and looked tired enough to pass out on the spot.

"Well, what do you think?" Vince asked.

She let out a deep breath. "I think he'll be all right. It's going to take a while to heal, but the bullet is out. I've done all I can to make him comfortable."

Vince slid off the hood and walked over to her and Cy. He put his hand on Reese's shoulder and looked her in the eye. "We're lucky to have you with us," he said. "I'm proud of you. You did a good job tonight, both of you." Vince glanced over at Cy.

Reese caught him off guard and gave him a hug as she began to cry. She hung on for a minute before letting go and stepping back. She wiped her tears away and forced a smile. "Sorry about that," she said with a laugh.

"Hey, there's nothing to be sorry about," Vince said. "We've all been through a lot. No plans for tomorrow morning. How about that? Sleep as long as you like."

Cy grabbed his dad's arm and looked at his watch. "It is tomorrow morning," he joked.

Vince smiled. "Right. Now go and get some rest. We'll have a decent meal when we're all up tomorrow."

Reese nodded and headed for her room with Buster in tow. Vince and Cy started for their rooms.

Vince squeezed Cy's shoulder. "How are you holdin' up?"

"I'm good. Just tired, you know?"

"I know. Trust me, I know."

They stopped at the door to Vince's room, and Cy put his arm around him for a second and squeezed. "Get some rest," Cy said. "I'll see you in a bit."

"I love you, Cy."

"I love you, too, Dad."

· 14 ·

When Vince entered the room, Mary was already sitting upright on the bed with Nugget at her side.

"Long day, huh?" Mary said.

Vince sighed. "The longest one I've had in a while."

"Do you think they'll retaliate? The looters?"

"Oh, I have no doubt they will when they figure out what's going on." Vince collapsed into the chair and began taking off his boots.

"Tonight?" she asked.

"I don't think so. At least I hope not. We did a lot of damage to their vehicles. They only have a few running cars and trucks we couldn't get to. Not to mention we took out five more of their guys, and I think they're going to sober up to the fact that we mean business. I'm willing to bet their next attack will be well planned out." That was exactly what worried Vince the most right now.

"How many of them are there?" Mary lay back in the bed.

"I don't know. I'm guessing originally there may have been as many as thirty or forty. There were a lot of vehicles around their place. I think they're a motorcycle gang or something like that, judging by the amount of bikes." Vince forced himself out of the chair and went to the bathroom to clean up a little. He set the lantern down on the vanity and took a good look at himself in the mirror.

"Wow." It came out louder than he intended, but he was shocked at how rough he looked.

"You okay in there?" Mary called from the other side of the door.

"Yeah, I guess I look about like I feel." Vince rubbed at his beard.

"We're all looking a little rough these days. I won't hold it against you," she joked.

Vince knew that powering the motel would be more important than he originally thought. They all needed to clean up and do laundry. For the time being, he was glad there weren't any more survivors as far as the supplies went, but they sure could have used more hands to help with the things that needed to get done around here.

They were going to have to split up tomorrow; there was no way around it. They would still have to keep a person on watch at all times, but everyone else was going to have to chip in. Depending on how Tom was doing, he might have to camp out in the truck all day. With his arm out of commission, he wouldn't be good for much else, but hopefully he'd be well enough to at least stand watch through several shifts and cover for the more able-bodied among them.

Vince finished cleaning up as best as he could with water and an already dirty towel, then dimmed the lantern. When he came out of the bathroom, Mary was half sitting up in bed and fast asleep. Nugget lifted her head to watch Vince as he tried to quietly make his way over to the other bed and lie down. When she realized Vince wasn't going anywhere, she put her head back down and settled in next to Mary, closing her eyes immediately. They were all tired, even the animals.

Vince thought about Mary's house and the animals there. Yet another thing that needed to happen sooner rather than later. He heard the pickup door slam outside and knew that it was around 6:00 a.m. without looking at his watch. Fred was relieving Bill from his watch duties. Traces of light seeped in from the edges of the curtains. Vince had hoped to be waking up about now to get a start on the day. Going out to Mary's house and rounding up the animals was the first thing on his list. *Was.* The word repeated in his mind. Instead, they would be beefing up defenses and taking precautions to defend against another attack, which was undoubtedly coming. When and how was anybody's guess.

He tried to quiet his thoughts but it wasn't working, and for as tired as he was, he couldn't sleep. He was too keyed up from the rescue, and he couldn't stop thinking about what they had done to get Ryan back. It wasn't the first time he had dealt with these feelings of guilt, but it had been a long time. As deserving as the looters were of retaliation, killing was still by no means enjoyable.

But even more than what he had done, he worried about John; they had been friends for a long time, and Vince considered them to be close. John had children later in life, too, just like Vince, and they had a lot in common. Vince had always related to John on many levels, but that was changing. The loss of his family had obviously taken its toll on him, but there was something else Vince couldn't quite put his finger on. Or maybe he was just overthinking it. Who among them hadn't changed in the last five days?

Even before he took out the kid who was guarding Ryan, John had been uncharacteristically quiet and seemed distant. And then there was the way that he had killed the last looter; he showed no emotion whatsoever. Vince pictured John standing in his store with a cup of coffee in his hand, smiling and giving Vince a hard time about Mary the way he did a few times each week. Vince wondered if he would ever see that version of John again.

And if all this was affecting a man like John, someone Vince held in high regard and considered about as tough and solid as they came, what did it mean for the rest of them? What about Cy? How was he really coping with all this? He was good at keeping things to himself, and Vince wondered if secretly he was barely hanging on. Cy made little jokes about things, and that was his way, but it was also how he dealt with stress. He hated that his son had to go through this, but there was nothing he could do about it. None of them could.

Vince tried to focus on taking a few deep breaths and calming himself down before he settled into bed. He glanced over at Nugget, who was curled up in a tight ball and snoring loudly. What he wouldn't give for a moment of ignorance about the world around them.

· 15 ·

Vince awoke to an empty room. The curtains were still pulled together, but several strong beams of light shone through the edges of the window and illuminated the floating dust particles in the room. He was surprised at the intensity of the light, and it was enough to coax him out of bed so he could see for himself.

He rose slowly and sat at the edge of the bed for a moment, trying to give his aching muscles a chance to accept what he was about to ask of them. According to his watch, he had slept for nearly six hours, and it was pushing noon. He took a couple of pills from the nightstand and washed them down with a half-full glass of room-temperature water before forcing himself to stand up.

Still half asleep, he stumbled over to the window and pulled one side of the curtains back a few inches. Squinting as the sunlight blasted him, he immediately felt the heat on his face and stepped back into the shadows. It was time to confront another day whether he liked it or not. He could have easily climbed back into bed and slept for a few more hours, but there was too much to do. He splashed a little water on his face and did his best to get himself together before he headed out.

As he stepped outside the room, the sun hit him full force, and the heat of the day seemed to seep into his soul. It was brighter than it had ever been since the EMPs, but the sky still retained its yellow tint. There was a noticeable lack of smoke and the stench that had plagued them for so long. A slight breeze blew past, and although warm, it was enough to make the air feel almost refreshing. For the first time in a week, Vince took a deep breath that didn't result in the urge to cough. He started to feel cautiously optimistic about the day and the possibilities of getting a few things done or at least well underway.

Hannah was sitting in the truck and waved at Vince when she saw him. "They're all in the dining room eating."

"Thanks." Vince waved back, still squinting as his eyes adjusted. He made his way down the covered walkway and past the other rooms. As he walked, he stared into the sky, searching for a hint of blue among the haze and clouds. The aroma of freshly brewed coffee and cinnamon struck him when he entered the door to the motel office. The smell was motivation enough to pick up his pace.

On the table was a large serving bowl of oatmeal. Next to it was a disposable foil tray with buttered and jellied toast stacked high. Finishing off the spread was a bowl full of canned peaches and two carafes of freshly brewed coffee.

"Hey there. Just in time," Cy said, smiling. Most everyone was there and had apparently just started eating. Vince was glad to see Ryan among them. He still clung to his mother, but that was nothing new. The boy seemed focused on the table full of food as if all that had happened last night was only a bad dream. Bill was absent, but that was to be expected after the midnight to 6:00 a.m. watch. Tom was also missing from the group, but that didn't come as a surprise, either. The one person that wasn't there but should have been was John, and that worried Vince.

"Good morning," Mary said. "I didn't want to wake you up. You were sleeping so well."

"Help yourself, Major," Sarah added.

"I didn't mean to sleep so long." Vince felt guilty, although he knew he had no reason to.

"You needed it. Besides, none of us have been up very long." Mary winked at him. Vince didn't waste any time and took his place in line. He hadn't realized how hungry he was until just now. His stomach growled as he stared at the food laid out on the table, but more than anything, he wanted a cup of coffee.

"Go ahead, Major. You guys earned it last night." Beverly smiled and stepped aside so he could move up in line.

"Nonsense. We all earned it. I'll wait my turn," he insisted.

Beverly smiled and stepped back into line, then turned around. "Thank you." She was about to say something else but stopped in order to fight back tears.

Vince nodded and put his hand on her shoulder. "We're all in this together. Now let's keep this line moving. I need some coffee," he joked.

No one said much else as they filled their paper plates with food and found spots to sit and eat. Vince watched Nugget sitting patiently at Mary's side and keeping an ever-watchful eye on every bit of food that left her plate.

"Such a beggar, but I don't think I have anything you would like," Mary teased.

"Where's Buster?" Vince looked at Reese.

"Oh, he's in the room. He gets a little pushy around food. Besides, he already ate."

"Well as long as he's taken care of," Vince said. "That's a heck of a dog you got there."

Reese smiled. "Thanks."

Beverly fixed a plate and headed out. "I'll go see if Tom is up. Maybe he'll be hungry."

Suddenly, Vince felt like a jerk. At the sight of the food, he had forgotten about pretty much everything outside the room.

"How is Tom?" Vince asked.

"It was a rough morning, but he finally fell asleep when the pain medicine kicked in."

"I'll stop in and see him later. He was a big help last night." Vince didn't have the heart to tell her the truth about how Tom almost got them all killed. She was already worried about her husband, and there was nothing to be gained by being honest at the moment. "Where's John? Anybody seen him this morning?" Vince asked.

"I knocked on his door and he said he'll be along in a bit," Mary answered.

"So what's the plan today, Major?" Fred asked.

Vince swallowed his coffee and thought for a second. The question caught him off guard, and he hadn't expected anyone to be anxious to do much of anything right away. But apparently the others were ready to work, and they were looking to him for direction.

"Well, we need to get supplies from the outdoor section at Mary's store and build out the courtyard here to accommodate animals. Once that's ready, I'd like to send a team to her house and gather up the surviving livestock and bring them here. Reese, I'd like you to be a part of that effort. Some of those animals may need medical attention. They've been living on their own for a week now." Vince looked at Mary.

"They're all scavengers and can live off the land for a while," Mary said. "The only ones I'm really worried about are the pigs. They have access to the barn, and I'm hoping they'd break into the feed bags if they got hungry enough. They've done it before." She shook her head.

"You guys can take the Ford pickup," Vince continued. "There's no need to use that to stand watch shifts in anymore. We've got plenty of other options, and that pickup will easily tow Mary's old horse trailer. You should be able to get all the animals at once, don't you think?"

Mary made a face at Vince. "It'll be interesting, but I suppose we can squeeze them all in."

"I'll go with you guys and help out." Fred looked at Mary and then at Reese. Vince was going to ask Fred to come along with him, but he decided it was probably a good idea for Reese to spend some time with her dad. Besides, if Cy and John could help him out and then maybe Bill when he woke up later, that would be all the manpower they needed for what he wanted to do.

"What about the rest of us?" Cy asked.

"How about you, me, and John focus on building a perimeter out of the vehicles from the dealership, like we talked about. Bill can help us out, too, when he's up." Vince checked his watch.

He was really starting to worry about John.

Cy nodded. "Sounds good."

"Beverly and Sarah can stay back with the kids and look after Tom if he needs anything. Maybe help you guys out with the animals when you bring them back." Vince figured that Hannah might as well stay on watch duty. One of the other ladies could relieve her later. He also thought the kids would enjoy helping out with the animals, and it might provide a welcome distraction for them.

Reese looked around the room. "Everyone remember to take water with you today. We don't want anybody getting dehydrated."

"She's right," Vince added. "Everybody is responsible for carrying their own water today. Fill up your bottles and take them with you." The last thing Reese needed was a patient with heat stroke, and there was no doubt that it would be a concern today. Vince had worked up a small sweat just walking from his room to here. They were going to have to pace themselves or none of them would last very long. But at least the air quality was better and would make life a little easier as they went about their jobs.

As they all started to filter out and head back to their rooms in order to prepare for the hard day ahead, Fred approached Vince and pulled him aside.

"What about the looters?" he asked in a hushed voice.

"We're just going to have to see what happens. We can't wait around on our butts for them to show up."

Fred sighed. "Yeah, I know."

"We have the radios, and with any luck, the clearer air will give us more range and allow us to stay in touch with whoever's on watch." This reminded Vince of something he wanted to say before everyone was gone. "Weapons," he called out. "Don't forget to carry your weapons at all times."

Everyone nodded and then left the room. Fred, apparently satisfied with Vince's answer about the looters, followed the others. Mary had made a plate of food for John as she cleaned up the dining room.

"I'll take it to him," Vince said, grabbing the plate from Mary. He needed to fill his water bottles and pack his bag for the day, but first he needed to check on John.

· 16 ·

For the first time since they had all been staying at the motel, Vince saw open windows and doors as he walked past the rooms. The improved air quality was a break they all needed and deserved.

Vince paused at Tom and Beverly's room and stuck his head in the door. Ryan was sitting at the table, drawing on a piece of paper with a pen, while Beverly sat next to him and watched. Tom was sitting up in bed and furiously shoveling food into his mouth with his good arm. He noticed Vince after a couple of seconds and looked embarrassed.

"Don't let me stop you. I just wanted to check in and see how you were doing."

"It hurts, but I'll survive," Tom joked. "I can manage if you need me."

"Nope, not today. Rest up and feel better. That's all I want you to do today. There'll be plenty for you to help us with when you've got your strength back." Vince started to walk away but stopped when Tom called out to him.

"Major, thank you."

Vince nodded. "Make sure he rests." He glanced at Beverly before moving on from the doorway. He'd talk to Tom about pulling extra watch duties some other time. For now, he needed to rest and regain his strength.

As he passed by the partially open doors, he noticed everyone was busy getting ready. Buster and Nugget had taken advantage of the situation and were making their way in and out of various rooms as they followed one another around. The two dogs were obviously excited by the activity and curiously checked in with everyone as they made their rounds.

When Vince reached John's room, the door was closed, and so was his window. He wondered if John had even been outside today. Vince knocked on the door and waited.

"Yeah?" John answered after a few seconds.

"Hey, it's me, Vince. I brought you some food."

"It's open."

Vince opened the door slowly and struggled to see into the room as his eyes adjusted to the darkness. The curtains were still drawn, and other than a few thin rays of light, the room was pitch black.

"It's like a cave in here," Vince said. John was sitting at the edge of the bed with his head in his hands. As Vince entered and set the plate of food down next to him, he looked up. Vince took a seat on the bed across from him. John looked rough, like he hadn't gotten much sleep. Then again, they all kind of looked that way.

"You should step out and get some fresh air. It's decent today. Actually, better than decent. It's pretty good." The room was musty and dank, and Vince wondered if his room felt the same but he hadn't noticed. John eyed the food but left it on the bed next to him.

Vince was going to have to motivate John to break out of his funk. He wasn't discounting all that he had been through, but the food and a change of scenery were what John needed most right now.

Vince stood and walked over to the window, where he proceeded to part both curtains in one swift motion.

"Ugh," John grumbled as he turned away from the blast of sunlight. Vince opened the window and felt an instant influx of fresh air. John must have felt it, too; he turned his head toward the window and held up his hand to block the light as he attempted to look outside.

"It does look a little better," John admitted reluctantly.

"It's a lot better. Why don't you eat and get cleaned up and then join us outside? I want to get started on that wall today," Vince said.

"Yeah, all right. I'm moving." John sighed as he stood up slowly. "Give me a few minutes."

"All right then." Satisfied that John was on his feet, Vince left him to get ready, making sure to leave his door open as he exited the room. Fresh air and a change of scenery weren't going to fix his friend, but for the time being, they would provide a measure of relief. Still, Vince would have to keep a close eye on John for a while. He couldn't afford to lose him. None of them could. Not that they could afford to lose anyone in their small group, but John was someone Vince could depend on when the going got tough. Hopefully, that would remain the case.

Within fifteen or twenty minutes, most everyone that was heading out on a project had assembled in the motel parking lot. Vince filled Sarah in on what was going on and told her to have Bill drive his truck to the Chevy dealership when he was feeling up to it.

Vince and his team would take the radio since they were going the farthest from town. Mary and her crew would stick around the motel for the first part of the day as they prepared an enclosure for her chickens, ducks, goats, and pigs.

They swapped the Ford pickup with the newly acquired Lincoln Continental, and Mary, Reese, and her dad loaded up the truck with their things and climbed in. Buster let out a pitiful bark as he watched through the screen on the motel room window. Reese had opted to leave him behind today, figuring he would most likely chase Mary's animals rather than help round them up. They had Nugget with them to help with that. The little dog seemed pleased to be going solo today. Standing tall with her front paws perched on the rail of the truck bed, she all but ignored Buster's yelps and whines.

The other day, Vince had cleared the debris from around Mary's store so that the outdoor area of her place was accessible. They'd have more than enough supplies and fencing to close off the small openings in the courtyard. Vince figured that it wouldn't take them more than an hour to prep it for the animals. They were only going to secure it for the time being, so they would put more time into something permanent later.

While Mary's team was prepping the courtyard, Vince and his team would head out of town to the car dealership. He would run the loader while Cy and John followed behind in John's Bronco. The dealership and Mary's house were in the same direction, and Vince planned on driving most of the way to her place in the loader to make sure they had clear roads. There was no need to go all the way out to her house. He just needed to make sure there was an open route through the denser neighborhoods.

His biggest concern was the sections of town with toppled houses covering the roads. The day the EMPs hit, he and Mary had barely escaped with their lives, and he knew firsthand that there were some impassable sections. Once he cleared the roads and there was enough room for them to get through, Mary would have no trouble driving to her place, other than the occasional wreck. Then he and his team would be free to head out to the Chevy dealership.

As they prepared to head out from the motel, the looters were never far from Vince's thoughts. Splitting up like this made him feel exposed and paranoid. But what choice did they have? What he told Fred was true. They couldn't afford to sit around and wait for the next attack. Survival was about being proactive and taking action, and now was as good of a time as any. They had severely handicapped the looters. It would be foolish not to capitalize on this opportunity. They had a few cars and four-wheelers left, but Vince reckoned they wouldn't attack in small numbers next time they came.

It was a double-edged sword. Vince felt like he had some time before the looters attacked next, but it wouldn't last long. When they did come again, he had no doubt that they would come with everything they had.

· 17 ·

The roads in the densely built neighborhoods weren't as bad as Vince had expected. The narrower streets and tightly packed houses meant that practically everything had burned to the ground and the streets were blocked. But the debris from the collapsed houses had been reduced to nothing more than ash and charred wood. The loader easily cleared it away, and since they weren't trying to accomplish anything other than making the roads passable for Mary and the others, it didn't take much time at all. The only thing that took a little effort was pushing the burned-out cars off the road, but there weren't many of those to deal with.

Once the roads were clear and Vince was sure that Mary wouldn't have any trouble driving out to her place, John radioed the motel and let the others know they were good to go. With the roads cleared, they were free to make their way out to the Chevy dealership.

The dealership was just on the outskirts of town and no more than five miles from the motel. Of course, they could only go as fast as the loader and the roads would allow them. The roads weren't too bad, but there was the occasional wreck to deal with. Unfortunately, most of the vehicles on the road when the EMPs hit were delivery trucks making their early-morning rounds, so the wrecks they did come across were substantial.

It was worth taking the time now to clear these trucks off the roadway. Although it wasn't difficult to drive around some of them as they were, Vince knew that the trip back from the dealership would be a different story. If things went according to plan, they'd be towing vehicles, and navigating the obstacles on the road would be much more challenging.

He hoped they could find an intact car carrier, the type that would normally be towed by a semi truck and could hold several vehicles. The dealership usually had one or two parked out back. The loader would have enough torque to pull the trailer—at least he hoped it did. Hooking the trailer to the loader would be a challenge, but not one they couldn't handle. Vince brought along a few sections of heavy-duty tow chain from his garage as well as a good assortment of tools.

The process wouldn't be easy, and it wouldn't be fast, but if they could move at least five cars at a time, he would be happy with that. All in all, he figured that building the wall would take them a few days at least. The most important part of the perimeter would be the front and the rear entrances.

They needed to use new cars in those two locations to allow for quick entry and exit from the perimeter. He reckoned they would use a pair of Chevy Suburbans as a gate. While none of the new cars would run, they could be easily pushed or pulled by one of their working vehicles.

Weight was another reason to use new vehicles where the wall would likely see the most action. The wrecks he had placed across the road with the loader to form the current barrier were burned-out shells. They didn't weigh much at all, and he suspected that a vehicle could ram its way through with a direct hit. The ramming vehicle would sustain major damage, but it would certainly make it through and open a hole that other cars could then use to gain access to town.

The new vehicles would be heavy, and with their tires still intact, they would offer far more resistance if rammed. Vince wasn't opposed to stacking the cars two or three high in places he wanted to be more permanent. In those areas, he also planned to let the air out of the tires in order to make it more difficult for a person to crawl under the wall.

Building a wall out of cars would be no small feat, but it would be well worth the peace of mind. Fearing the constant threat of an attack was no way to live. The wall would also provide a very defensible position. Unlike before, when he and John were pinned down behind the two-car roadblock, they would be able to move along the cars in either direction during an attack. That would be a huge advantage in a gunfight.

John and Cy had driven up ahead in the Bronco to scout the road out for Vince. He had lost sight of them temporarily, but now he saw the Bronco headed back his way. John pulled up next to the loader and waited for Vince to open the door to the cab.

"What's up?" Vince shouted over the diesel engine.

John shook his head. "Big mess up at the intersection on Boone Street and Main. Big truck, all the way across the road."

Vince nodded and pulled the door closed while John pulled away and took a position behind the loader once more. It must have been pretty bad if John couldn't get around it. When Vince came around the corner, he laid eyes on the remains of the eighteen-wheeler.

The truck and trailer were stretched horizontally across the road, almost like it had been put there on purpose. The rear of the truck was wedged against a metal overhead light pole, and the front end was partially embedded into what was left of a burned-out building. It couldn't have happened at a worse location, as this was probably the narrowest section of Main Street in the older downtown area. There wasn't even enough room for a person to squeeze by on the sidewalk at either end.

Vince considered leaving it in place and using the side streets, but he abandoned that idea when he thought about how hard it would be to navigate a large trailer on the even tighter back roads through town. No, they needed to move this off the road and out of the way. Besides, going the back way to the car dealership would take too long and add a lot of extra work to an already complicated process.

Vince lowered the bucket on the loader as he squared up on the truck and attempted to push it off the light pole. Black smoke poured out of the loader's exhaust stack as the diesel roared. The noise was deafening, even inside the enclosed cab. He throttled the big machine up as much as he dared, but he wasn't moving, and neither was the truck.

"Come on," Vince grumbled. He let off the pedal and let the RPMs drop back to idle before he backed up a few feet. He didn't want to risk blowing any seals or hydraulic lines. They needed the road cleared, but they needed the loader more.

"Come on. Think this through for a second. Work smart," Vince said out loud as he studied the truck. It was a logging truck—or at least it used to be—and by the looks of the ash and charcoal, it had been carrying a full load. The only thing that remained was the trailer's heavy-duty steel framework with its upright supports and cross members.

Vince could see all the way through to the clear road on the opposite side, only adding to the frustration of it all. To make matters worse, the light pole at the back of the truck was bent from the heat of the fire, he assumed, and leaned into the steel framework of the trailer, preventing him from pushing the back end out of the way.

He was going to have to concentrate on the front end near the cab. That was something he had hoped to avoid, mostly because he didn't want to find the driver but also because it was several feet into a large pile of debris that had once been a brick building. It was the old bank, and it had collapsed around the front end of the truck, burying most of the cab in brick and charred timbers.

There was no other way this was going to work, so Vince stopped trying to overthink the situation and began the tedious process of removing the debris bucket by bucket. After he had removed a few buckets full of brick from the bottom of the pile, the remainder of the rubble fell away from the truck, exposing the crushed cab and what was left of its occupant.

A bloody and mangled arm, pinched between the truck's caved-in roof and the top of the door, protruded from the driver's seat. Vince tried his best to ignore the gruesome sight, but it was hard. Each time he came into contact with the pile of debris, it shook the truck, causing the arm to dangle back and forth.

He worked as quickly as he could, and as soon as he thought that enough of the pile was cleared, he made another attempt to move the truck. This time it worked, and the truck began to pivot on the light pole. He could hear the steel groan over the diesel as the metal bent and gave in to the loader.

The dangling arm swung from the window, taunting him the whole way. It was directly in front of Vince and impossible not to notice as the truck cab contorted and twisted under the pressure of the loader. Just when he thought it couldn't get any worse, the bone snapped, causing the arm to fall off and land on top of the loader bucket. Vince was disgusted at the sight and swore he could hear it land, even though he knew that was impossible.

He forced himself to look away and checked over his shoulder to see where John and Cy were. Cy gave him a thumbs-up from the Bronco, blissfully unaware of what Vince had just seen.

Finally, Vince had the bulk of the truck off the

road and onto the opposite sidewalk. He pushed it a few more feet for good measure before letting off the pressure and raising the bucket up far enough to tip it. The arm rolled off the bucket and disappeared into the remains of the truck. He refused to look at the truck as he backed away. John and Cy sped by in the Bronco and resumed scouting the road ahead.

Vince was glad to get away from there and tried to think about Mary and the others. He hoped they were making good progress and were heading out to retrieve the animals by now. Mary had her doubts about the pigs' survival, but even if they only managed to save the chickens, ducks, and goats, that would be a huge win for them all. As long as the animals were fed and taken care of, they would provide a renewable resource of eggs and milk.

A few minutes had passed when Vince spotted the Bronco returning once again. His heart sank as he imagined another blockage up ahead. John passed the loader this time, though, and made a U-turn, then eventually pulled up so that the passenger side of the Bronco was closest to the loader. Cy leaned out the window as Vince reluctantly opened the cab door and braced for the bad news.

"It's all clear," Cy reported. "All the way to the dealership."

"Glad to hear that," Vince said.

"We'll run up ahead and have a look around. See you there." Cy waved as they pulled away. It was about time they caught a little break. They might actually accomplish something today. Vince watched as the Bronco drove off and disappeared. He had to admit that seeing them go on without him made him nervous. Vince pushed down on the throttle a little bit more as he told himself they'd be fine and that he'd join them in a couple of minutes.

· 18 ·

As Mary pulled up to what was left of her hardware store, she couldn't help but reminisce about better days. She hated that the store had been reduced to a pile of charred debris. There was a time in her life when the store was all she had. Or at least it had felt that way. After her husband passed, it was the only thing that kept her going at times. It had given her a purpose in life and a reason to force herself out of bed and keep moving forward. And now it was gone.

She wanted to be more upset about it, but she felt foolish every time she started to give in to the ugly feeling of self-pity. She might have lost her store, but compared to a lot of people, she was extremely lucky. For starters, she was alive and her house had survived the EMP surge. She had her friends, and she had Vince and of course Nugget. She was concerned about her daughter in Florida, but she had made peace with the fact that her daughter was okay.

Mary's daughter lived in southern Florida, where she and her husband operated a citrus grove and small farm. They were fairly self-sufficient and ran the majority of their operation on solar power. If the solar power system had saved Mary's house, it stood to reason that it would be the same for her daughter. And someday, whether it be two months from now or two years from now, they would see each other again. That was what her gut told her, and she believed it with all her heart. She had to.

Mary considered the possibility of traveling to Florida to find her daughter, but she wasn't willing to make a trip like that alone. And she didn't think it was right to ask Vince to go with her. Besides, they had their hands full in Cloverdale right now. Maybe if things took a turn for the worse here or if this coming winter proved too difficult with limited supplies, she would bring it up. These were some of the thoughts at the back of her mind, but she didn't dare dwell on them out of fear they would become reality.

"All right, girl, you stay put. We don't need you cutting your paw on anything." Mary scratched Nugget's head as she moved her to the cab of the truck. Nugget whined and immediately filled the vacant driver's seat as Mary closed the door.

"That's a good idea." Reese kicked at something on the ground, and a small charred piece of metal skittered across the concrete. "There's all kinds of junk on the ground," she added.

Vince had done a good job of clearing a path through the remains of the hardware store and to the outdoor lumber yard, but there was a lot of small debris left on the ground. The last thing Mary wanted was for Nugget to get hurt wandering around in the rubble.

Mary, Reese, and Fred picked their way down the roughly cleared path to the rear of the property. Mary glanced back at the truck to see Nugget. She had her front paws up on the dashboard as she watched them leave. The little dog would get to help out soon enough when they went to Mary's. Buster had risen to the occasion by tracking the kidnappers; it was Nugget's turn to help out next.

Building the sections of gate to keep the animals restricted to the motel courtyard was the easy part. The hard part would be rounding them up, but that was where Nugget came in. The chickens posed the biggest problem, and after all that had happened, they were bound to be a little skittish. Of course, none of this would matter if there were no animals.

The thought had crossed her mind many times over the past week. What if they were all dead? It was possible. She thought about the air quality and the lack of food and possibly water. It had been so hot and dry since the EMPs that there was a very real possibility the animals had become dehydrated.

Luckily, she had filled the large water trough early in the morning last Sunday, before everything happened. But she still worried if it was enough.

As they wandered around the outdoor supply yard and gathered materials, she tried not to think about the animals too much. Honestly, she was afraid to get her hopes up about what they might find at her house. Was her house even still standing?

She thought back to the out-of-control inferno that had engulfed what had once been a quaint little neighborhood. She and Vince nearly ended up trapped. How far would the fire spread if left unchecked by the fire department? The wheat had been cut on the property adjacent to hers, but a grass fire was still possible. She tried to prepare herself for the worst-case scenario, but deep down, she wasn't willing to accept the possibility of a total loss.

They picked their way around the lumber yard and managed to gather a post-driver, a roll of galvanized wire fence, and enough metal fence posts to make do for now. There would be time to perfect the setup later. Right now, she was anxious to gather the animals. Once they were settled, she could come back and pick up more supplies. They still needed a watering and feeding trough along with the surplus bags of feed she kept locked up in the shed out back.

She originally kept the feed in the store, but it attracted too many mice, especially during the winter months. It never seemed to bother her husband when he ran things, but seeing the dead mice in the traps disgusted her. So one of the first things she did when she took over was move all the animal feed outdoors. She had a weather-tight shed built just for that purpose. And now, thanks to that decision, all the feed had survived the fire and would keep the animals fed for quite some time.

With the back of the truck loaded, they drove back to the motel and started working on the enclosure. Having finished sleeping in after his midnight to 6:00 a.m. watch, Bill gave them a hand unloading the truck.

The motel building formed an almost complete enclosure on its own, creating an open courtyard at the center. The area was rectangular in shape and had two points of access from outside. Overall, it was probably close to one hundred feet in length by at least fifty feet wide. This would be a much smaller space than the animals were used to, but they would have to make do for their own good.

One of the access points was a covered passageway next to the motel office. A break in the building ran all the way through to the yard, separating the first guest room from the office, dining room, and kitchen via a ten-foot-wide walkway. There was another similar spot at the other end of the building. The two access points were connected by an S-shaped path of stepping stones through the otherwise grass-covered yard. Within each one of these covered walkways was an ice machine and a couple of vending machines.

Rather than move them out of the way, Bill had the idea to use them as part of the barrier, so they lined them up as best as they could to block off half of the access points. As they moved the empty vending machines, Mary stared through the glass and thought about how they had all pretty much lived off the contents for the first three days. It seemed like such a long time ago, and when she thought about how little time had actually passed, it seemed impossible. She hoped they would never have to eat like that again.

The soda machines were a different story. They were heavy and still full, but only because they couldn't find the key anywhere and nobody wanted to break into them. Plus, now they had plenty of fresh water. The thought of drinking a hot soda was less than appealing. They'd open them up at some point, but for now, it was low on the list of things to do.

With the vending machines and ice machines moved to the back of each access point and along the edge of the concrete walkway, they now had to close the remaining gap with fencing. The dirt was hard and dry from the baking sun, and it took Fred and Bill's combined efforts to drive the posts into the ground. While they took turns using the post-driver, Mary and Reese measured and cut sections of fence off the roll with a pair of bolt-cutters from Vince's garage.

They closed off the farthest access from the office first, without using any type of gate. Mary figured it was far enough away from any of the rooms they were living in and wasn't worth the risk. She reasoned with the others that building a gate on that side would be a waste of time right now and would only serve as a possible escape point for the animals.

Her real reason, however, was rooted in fear— fear that someone could sneak in from that side of the building in the middle of the night and steal the animals. If the looters found out they had livestock, there would be even more reason to attack them. Not that the looters seemed to need any more motivation, but why make it easy? These animals would be the most valuable things they had, and protecting them might mean the difference between life and death for her and the others.

She hated to think about things in absolutes, but these were the days of ultimatums. There was no such thing as trying anymore. There was success or there was failure. Their lives now did not forgive foolish mistakes, and just about every decision they made would determine their fate as a team, like it or not.

Mary still missed her husband, but part of her was glad he wasn't around to see the world this way.

· 19 ·

When Vince finally reached the Chevy dealership, he spotted John's old Bronco right away since the boxy pale-blue shape of the classic SUV stood out among the rows of sleek, shiny vehicles. Vince pulled the loader up next to John's truck and shut it down. It felt good to get out of the stuffy cabin, and he stretched as he exited.

The loader's ventilation system wasn't working, and even though he had intermittently held the cab door open with his foot during the trip, it did little to cool him down. They had barely started today, and his back was already soaking wet with sweat from being trapped against the black vinyl seat.

From his spot in the loader, he could see above the rows of new cars and had a commanding view of the property. The showroom was destroyed, as he expected, but the workshop in the back of the property was a separate building and surprisingly still intact. Vince wondered if it was powered by a subpanel and had therefore been saved when the circuits overloaded and tripped at the main building.

He held his hand up to his forehead to block the glare from the sun as he looked around, but he couldn't locate his son or John. Where were they? He really wished they had waited for him instead of rushing ahead on their own. John and Cy were both capable; that wasn't his concern. He just didn't like not knowing what was going on. Vince was about to call out to them but decided against it so as to avoid drawing attention to himself, although he wasn't sure why. It wasn't like he had come in quietly on the big yellow loader.

Just as he was about to genuinely start worrying, Cy popped out from around the corner of the workshop and waved him over. The car lot was several acres in size, so Vince decided to drive the loader over to the building rather than walk. When he arrived at the outbuilding, he found John and Cy along the side. They were looking over a car carrier. It was the kind meant to be pulled by a semi truck, and it was what Vince had hoped to find here. Just the sight of the large trailer gave him hope that their plan might actually work.

He joined them on the ground as they inspected the trailer. Vince had limited knowledge of these large multicar transport systems. He owned a single-car flat-bed trailer that they used sparingly at his shop, but most of the time, they relied on an outside towing company to handle broken-down vehicles and their towing needs. Insurance for the garage was cheaper without offering a towing service, and it was a way to avoid any liability issues.

The trailer was fairly new, and Vince had seen ones like it loaded and unloaded more than a few times. Not having a semi to tow the trailer the way it was made to be towed meant they would also lose some of the functionality of the hauler, along with half its capacity. They would still be able to carry five or six vehicles at a time, depending on their size, but not being able to use the trailer's hydraulic system to raise and lower levels would limit them.

Vince did his best to share what he knew about the process with Cy and John, but the bigger problem was how they were going to tow this thing once it was loaded. The loader had a flat back and no hitch of any kind. Even if it had a hitch, it wouldn't have mated with the car carrier, which was set up for a tradition fifth wheel-style coupling on a semi truck. Vince knew the answer to the problem but desperately wanted to figure out another way, though there wasn't any choice in the matter.

They were going to have to lift the tongue of the trailer with the loader bucket and tow it backward.

They could use the heavy-duty tow chains Vince brought along as a safety precaution to make sure the trailer didn't slide off the bucket. It wouldn't be easy, but he couldn't think of any other realistic way to accomplish the task. It was already going to take a lot of time and effort to get the cars and trucks loaded.

John and Cy agreed with his idea, and they set about hooking the loader bucket to the front of the trailer before they started loading vehicles. It would be easier to test it out with an unloaded trailer. Plus, with the trailer hooked up, Vince could move it around the car lot to make loading the cars easier.

Getting the vehicles onto the trailer would present its own unique set of challenges. With the dealership showroom destroyed, the chance of finding keys to the cars was slim to none. Vince had a couple of tricks up his sleeve to put the vehicles into neutral so they could load them, but the cars would all be locked.

These were all modern vehicles and didn't have post-style locks, so the old slim jim method wouldn't work on them. He had planned for this, though, and as much as he hated to use it, he brought along an emergency glass hammer from the garage, and it was made specifically for breaking windows. The hammer would make a mess, so they'd have to be careful to avoid cutting themselves on thousands of tiny glass shards, but it was the quickest way to gain access.

Once he had access to the interior, he could shift the cars into neutral, but they would still have to deal with the steering. Without the key, they would be limited by how much they could actually steer the car—another good reason to bring the trailer. If they turned the wheel too far in either direction, the steering would lock and the car would have to be dragged into position before being loaded onto the trailer.

Nothing about this process would be easy, and it would take them the better part of the day and into the night, if they dared work that long. The return of the looters was never far from his mind.

John told Vince that he had tested the radio when he and Cy first arrived at the dealership, and it worked. It wasn't completely clear, but it was better than no communication at all. This gave Vince a little peace of mind, and if something came up and the others needed him, John, and Cy, they could at least get in touch. With the roads between the dealership and the motel cleared, they could all jump in John's Bronco and be back to the others within minutes.

Vince approached the front of the trailer and lined the bucket up with the center of the coupler as best as he could. Once he was in position, he slowly raised the bucket until he saw the trailer's landing gear lift from the blacktop. He was glad to see the loader handle the weight with ease. He'd had his doubts about the loader's ability, but so far so good. Of course, the trailer was empty; add a few SUVs and half-ton pickups and it might be a different story.

They wouldn't use the chains to tie it all together just yet because Vince thought they might need the loader to help line the cars up. They would chain them all together for the trip back. If the trailer slipped off the bucket while loaded down with vehicles, the weight would most likely bend the landing gear, and they might not be able to lift it back up if it was lying flat on the ground.

With the trailer tongue supported by the loader bucket, John and Cy cranked up the trailer's landing gear the rest of the way to provide extra clearance. Once they were clear, Vince began to back up slowly. The trailer slid out of the bucket with a terrible metallic scraping noise, and Vince thought he was going to lose it for a second.

He stomped on the brakes while tilting the bucket back as far as it would go. Luckily, the king pin caught on a piece of steel he had welded onto the forks for extra strength the other day. He let out a deep sigh of relief and started backing up again. This time, everything stayed put and the trailer began rolling forward. This might actually work.

· 20 ·

John and Cy walked alongside the trailer as Vince pulled it across the car lot. He headed for a row of SUVs and trucks near the front of the dealership, bypassing the smaller sedans; he was interested in the heavier vehicles right now. There was no telling how much they'd accomplish today, but he was determined to at least replace the current roadblock with a new system.

The lot comprised many tightly parked rows of cars, and unfortunately, he had to go straight through the middle of them to move the trailer to the front near the road. Vince sat sideways in the seat, doing his best to keep one eye on the trailer and the other on the back end of the loader, which was now technically the front. It was a lot like backing up a trailer. Add in the articulated steering and there were moments when he honestly didn't know which way to turn the wheel in order to force the unwieldy rig to comply.

He eventually started to get the hang of it and figure out how to move the trailer to where he wanted it to go. He picked up speed a little in an effort to move things along, but he cut his turn around a row of cars too sharply. John threw his hands up to warn him, but it was too late: the trailer clipped the last sedan in the row and dragged it along for a couple of feet before it fell away.

Vince shrugged at the mistake, but the trailer seemed unaffected by the collision, so he continued toward his destination. Careful to give the trailer a larger radius on the next turn, Vince pulled in behind the first row of vehicles.

John had a winch on the front of his Bronco, and the plan all along had been to winch the cars onto the trailer from the front. So before Vince stopped, he cut the wheel hard to the left, brought the loader into the beginning of a turn, and drove for a few more yards before stopping. With the loader angled to the side of the trailer tongue, there was now room for the Bronco to line up head-on with the front of the car carrier. They could run the winch cable over the top of the trailer and pull the cars straight up the ramp one by one, toward the Bronco and the front of the trailer.

Vince shut the loader off and joined Cy on the ground as John pulled his truck around and lined it up.

"Well, time to get to work, I guess." Cy looked at the nearest row of vehicles.

"Let's start with these." Vince walked toward a line of Chevy Suburbans. He approached the first one and set his tool bag down before he peered into the window. Vince scoffed as he glanced at the spec sheet in the window.

"What?" Cy asked.

"Over seventy-two thousand dollars." Vince shook his head. He never could wrap his head around the price they charged for new vehicles or how people could justify spending that kind of money on something to get you from point A to point B. Now the sticker seemed even more ridiculous than ever. He was basically looking at a seventy-thousand-dollar paperweight—or, in their case, roadblock.

"Yeah, well I hear they're giving them away today while supplies last," Cy joked.

Vince couldn't help but smile as he rooted through his bag for the glass hammer. He was about to pull back the hammer and take a swing when John came around the back of the truck.

"Whoa, hold it, hold it," John yelled.

"I've got to get inside. It has to be in neutral before we can move it," Vince explained.

"I've got a better way." John held up a bag of his own. He set it down and pulled out two small airbags and a long stick with a hook at one end.

"Watch this." John approached the driver's door and went to work.

The two small airbags were about the size of a person's hand, and they each had a clear tube attached to them with a ball-style hand pump. John took one of the uninflated bags and slid it between the door and the frame of the truck, forcing it under the weather stripping. Once it was in place, he gave the pump a couple of squeezes, and the bag forced the door about half an inch off the body as it swelled full of air. He repeated the process using the other bag at the top of the door, this time with the same result. Using the stick with a hook on it, he passed it into the small opening the bags had created and used the hooked end to activate the door handle. The door popped open and the bags fell to the ground.

"There you go." John stepped back. "All yours."

"Wow, that was easy," Cy said.

Vince was impressed with John's system. "That's a lot better than my way."

John smiled and picked the bags up off the ground. He twisted the release valve on the pump and let the air out, making the bags flat once more.

"Here you go. You can do the next one while I get the winch cable unrolled." John handed the bags and stick to Cy and headed back to his truck. Cy looked over the hood of the oversized SUV and glanced down the line of trucks.

"Which ones should I open?" Cy asked.

"Just work your way down the line. I want to grab at least four or five, maybe more if we can fit 'em." Vince was already inside the truck and working at getting the rubber boot off the base of the column shifter.

"Got it." Cy hurried to the next vehicle, leaving Vince to himself. Vince had worked on a few newer Chevys but none this new. On the trucks he'd seen, inside the column there was a release that was normally triggered when you inserted the key and allowed the lever to be shifted into gear. Without the key, he would have to manually push the pin back and out of the way in order to free the shifter up.

Pleased to see that the design hadn't changed on the newer models, he inserted a flathead screwdriver and pushed. Within seconds, he had the truck in neutral and had to put his foot on the brake to keep it from rolling down the slight incline of the car lot. He checked to make sure Cy was clear and that John was out of the way before he took his foot off the pedal.

The big Suburban inched backward, and he carefully turned the wheel. The truck backed out of its spot in a wide arc. Vince was careful not to turn the wheel too hard and lock it up. He could feel the spring tighten and held it as far to the left as he dared. If he went too far and the steering locked up, they'd be screwed and wouldn't be able to turn the vehicle without the key.

When he had backed up as far as he could without pushing the truck, he pulled the emergency brake and climbed out. He stepped back and looked at the angle of the truck in relation to the trailer ramp, and he was pleased with it. He was only about fifteen degrees from being lined up with the ramp, and once the winch cable was hooked up, steering onto the carrier should be no problem.

John was up on top of the trailer, fishing the winch cable through the frame and over the top of the rig. He pulled it through until he had enough slack to reach the Suburban.

"Heads up," John called out and tossed the cable off the end of the trailer to Vince. Once the Suburban was attached, John took his position at the front of the Bronco and prepared the winch by taking the slack out of the cable until it was tightly stretched over the carrier. Vince would have liked to have another radio for this operation and was relieved to see Cy heading over to join them.

"The whole row is unlocked." Cy looked back at the line of trucks proudly.

"Great, how about giving us a hand? You can relay messages in case I need him to stop winching. I can't use the windows and there isn't enough room on the ramp to keep the door open, so watch for my hand signals. Thumbs up: keep winching.

Closed fist: stop." Vince made a fist and held it up so Cy could see.

"No problem." Cy nodded and took a spot midway along the trailer on the other side so he could keep an eye on his dad and John at the same time. Vince climbed into the truck and did a quick check to make sure he wasn't forgetting anything. Satisfied that he had thought of everything, he released the emergency brake. The big SUV rolled back a few inches before being stopped by the cable. Vince closed the door and gave Cy a thumbs up.

Within a few seconds, Vince was moving toward the ramp on the back of the trailer. Careful not to over-steer and lock out the wheel, he lined up the tires with the two sections as best as he could. As the front tires rolled onto the ramp, Vince heard the trailer creak and groan as the weight of the Suburban settled in. He made a few minor adjustments to center the truck on the two narrow metal supports. It felt like the trailer was too narrow to accept the oversized SUV, but he kept rolling forward. Before he knew it, he was up on the top level of steel grates.

It was a lot higher than it looked from the ground, and it made Vince nervous to be perched up there on the thin steel planks that were just wide enough to fit the tires. When he reached the end of the ramp, he held up his fist and felt the truck slow its advance. He stopped it all the way by pressing down hard on the brake.

He set the emergency brake and flung the door open, forgetting about the rail that ran along the outside of the trailer. The door banged into the railing, and as he squeezed out through the slim opening, he eyed the large dent he had put in the new truck.

"Oops," he mumbled. Then he felt silly when it dawned on him that the dent was probably the nicest thing that would happen to this Suburban in the very near future.

Vince made his way around to the front of the truck and waited while John backed off the tension on the winch. When it was loose enough, he unhooked the cable and walked it back down the ramp to the parking lot.

Normally, after the first vehicle was loaded, the hydraulics would be used to adjust the ramps for the next vehicle, which would have been loaded under the Suburban. But without a proper tow vehicle to hook the trailer's utilities up, that wasn't an option. They would have to make do with the space on the top tier of ramps alone.

Once on the ground, Vince stepped back and eyeballed the remaining space. He was disappointed to see how much room the Suburban had taken up and figured they could only squeeze on three more at most. After they delivered this load of vehicles to the motel, he'd talk to John about hooking up the single-car trailer from his garage to the Bronco or maybe one of the other vehicles. It would only add one more vehicle per run to the dealership and back, but every bit counted. Either way, there was no getting around the fact that this was going to be a long, slow process.

· 21 ·

With the motel courtyard turned into a crude holding pen for the animals, Mary, Reese, and Nugget loaded into the Ford. They made a quick stop and checked in with Sarah, who had taken over watch duties for the afternoon shift and was now manning the radio. She let them know that Vince had cleared a path and that they should be good to go. Vince also suggested that Bill help them round up the animals at Mary's, as they had things under control at the car lot.

So Fred and Bill followed Mary and Reese in Bill's Dodge pickup; they figured an extra vehicle to help carry supplies from Mary's wouldn't hurt. The animals were the priority, but Mary had a lot of other things that she hoped to bring back to the motel. She wanted to get all she could in this first trip; there was no guarantee they would have the chance to go back again anytime soon, especially if the looters decided to show up.

She had her own shotgun and a few cartons of ammunition for it in her closet upstairs, but the main thing on her mind was her basement full of canned goods. Her stash of preserved items was probably equal to or greater than what they found at the grocery store. All those long hours of canning surplus vegetables were really going to pay off, and she was glad she could contribute in such a big way. At least she hoped she could, provided they had survived and her house was still there.

As they headed out of town, it was obvious where Vince had used the loader to clear a path for them. They still proceeded with caution, though; there was still plenty of smaller debris scattered on the road. Mary thought about the houses that had succumbed to the fires and tumbled onto the streets. The thought of picking up a nail and blowing a tire was reason enough to take their time and be careful.

Not a single house was left standing, and the once quaint community of historic homes reminded her more of a war zone she'd seen on the evening news than of the Cloverdale she knew and loved. She drove this route to her store nearly every day of the week, and now it was barely recognizable. She hated seeing all the piles of burned lumber and trash where houses had once stood. They had gone through slowly in part to be cautious but mainly because they were all mesmerized by the devastation.

Mary was glad to put the congested streets of what used to be a neighborhood behind them. As the landscape opened up to wheat fields and empty pastures, she picked up speed. She glanced in her rearview mirror to confirm that the men were still following. As she neared her house, it dawned on her that the pastures were eerily absent of animals. She really started to worry when she reached the Whittakers' farm. There were no horses grazing and no cows lounging in the shade at the edge of the trees.

The Whittakers were her closest neighbors. Their forty-plus-acre parcel of land was adjacent to her property, separated only by a small patch of woods. They kept several horses and a few token cows on their land. Mr Whittaker was a doctor in town, and he and his wife had two teenage children. Mary had taken them baked goods on many occasions, and they had reciprocated in kind.

The daughter rode horses and could often be seen riding in the pasture when Mary drove by on her way home from the store. Occasionally, if she happened by at the right time, the girl would race her horse against Mary in her Jeep, along the fence line that paralleled the road, but not today—and probably not ever again.

The Whittakers big two-story home was gone, burned to the ground. Nothing but a pile of charred remains sat at the end of the perfectly straight tree-lined driveway. Thankfully, they had been away on vacation. Mary hoped that wherever they were, they had escaped the fate of so many others. She took some comfort in knowing their bodies weren't among the rubble. The odds of them still being alive were slim, but she chose not to think about it anymore and turned her attention to the approaching tree line.

Her house would be visible soon, and the moment of truth was at hand. Had her house survived or burned down from an out-of-control grass fire that spread to her property? She'd seen many scorched fields on their journey out here today. She was on the edge of her seat as they cleared the trees, trying to catch a glimpse of her house.

It was still there, and she breathed a heavy sigh of relief as she slowed down and prepared to turn into the gravel drive. The feeling was temporary, however, as she thought about her animals. The fact that the Whittakers' field had lacked any signs of life gave her good reason to be concerned. Had the smoke killed them? Had they broken through the fence and ran from the flames in a moment of panic? It wouldn't be the first time the cows had escaped.

Mary was relieved to see her one and only rooster dart out from under her front porch and greet the approaching vehicles. Nugget began to become restless and whine as they neared the end of the driveway. She knew they were home, and it was probably the first thing that made sense to the little dog since they left a week ago.

Mary brought the truck to a stop next to her Jeep. Bill, along with a cloud of dust, pulled in beside her. They all unloaded and watched as Nugget tore after the rooster, chasing him back under the porch. Giving up on the rooster, Nugget launched into a fit of running at full speed and in big circles around the yard.

"You better save your energy, girl. We've got work to do," Mary said. Nugget stopped dead in her tracks and looked at Mary, tongue fully out and panting hard from her sudden burst of energy. Mary walked over to the porch and looked through the lattice underneath.

"One, two…three, four…five, six, seven. Seven chickens under here. The rest must be out back." A large fenced-in section in her back yard stretched all the way to her small barn The chickens had a coup out there as well, but sometimes they roosted under her porch for reasons she did not understand. She'd tried to discourage them from going under there and even put lattice around the perimeter to stop them, but they had long ago pecked a chicken-sized hole in it. At the moment, she didn't care and was glad at least half of her flock was safe and sound.

Mary was tempted to go into her house and have a look around, but she knew they needed to get the animals squared away first. She led the others around the side of her house and opened the gate to the fenced-in area.

Normally when she went out in the morning to feed the animals, they would run out from the barn to greet her. There was a hole in one of the large sliding barn doors, and it was big enough for the goats and pigs to use at their leisure so they could come and go as they pleased. On the door was a semitransparent heavy-duty plastic flap that helped keep the weather out, but it hung limp. There was no sign of movement as they approached.

Mary's heart sank as she began to face the reality that she might only have the seven chickens left. Then, suddenly, the flap lifted, and one after another, the goats came pouring out, followed by two pigs. They must have been hiding in there since this all started. She didn't blame them and would have done the same in their situation.

"There you are!" Mary wiped away tears of joy as the goats trotted over to greet them, bleating as they came. The pigs weren't far behind, and before long, a chicken pushed its way past the plastic flap as well.

"Well, they sure are glad to see you. Is this all of them?" Reese knelt as one of the goats approached her, but Mary didn't answer; she was too busy counting heads. A few were missing, and she hoped the rest were still inside the barn.

"Let's check in the barn. I'm missing a pig, the ducks, and a few chickens." Mary started for the big door, but Bill and Fred beat her to it and began pushing it open. She stood and watched as the light spilled in and illuminated the freshly kicked-up dust. In unison, four ducks stood up inside their nesting boxes as their midday nap was interrupted. They all began quacking in protest at the intrusion while Mary entered the barn and searched for the other animals. She found two of the missing chickens roosting in the loft area, but she was still short two birds and a pig.

"So I'm missing three chickens and a pig." She spun around and counted the animals again. The pigs were all adults and had some size to them. The chances of the other pig hiding somewhere were slim, and if it was here, it would have come running out with the others. No, something was wrong—something had happened to the missing pig and probably the chickens as well.

"There's one more place to check," Mary said half aloud. The fenced-in yard extended to one side of the barn where she kept the horse trailer and a few bales of straw. Anxious to figure out where the rest of the animals were, she made her way around as the others followed, but she wasn't prepared for what she found.

· 22 ·

There in the back corner of the yard was the missing sow — or at least what was left of her. Mary froze in her tracks as he tried to process what she was looking at. The pig wasn't just dead; it was torn apart.

Reese passed her and approached the carcass, then knelt to get a closer look. Mary joined her after a minute, and so did the others, although Mary was the only one to get down on the ground with Reese. What could have killed and butchered this animal like this? She immediately suspected foul play from people like the looters, but why was the body such a mess? If they killed it for meat, why didn't they take it with them?

"Someone or something sure made a mess of that poor thing." Fred crouched down near the pig to get a better look. Bill hung back several feet. He didn't seem too keen on having a closer look. Reese was investigating the carcass with a stick, poking and prodding some of the larger wounds.

"This was done by another animal." Reese pointed to a couple of different spots. "See there? And there? Teeth marks. Something with a pretty good bite radius. And it didn't happen that long ago. I'm guessing sometime last night or early this morning."

"What could have done that?" Bill glanced around at the empty fields surrounding them.

"We have a lot of coyotes around, but I can't see them taking on an animal this large unless it was a pack of them." Mary could see bite marks now that Reese had pointed them out. Over the years, she'd lost a chicken or two to coyotes, but never any large animals like this. The sow had to weigh close to three hundred pounds, if not more, and pigs could be aggressive when cornered or irritated. It just didn't make sense.

"It could have been a black bear, I guess. Look at these here. They could be claw marks." Reese pointed to another spot on the pig's back.

"A black bear? I've lived here all my life and never seen one." Fred stood up and looked around. "What would a bear be doing around here?" he added.

"They're not common, but I read that they've been making a comeback in the last few years," Mary said. A while back, an article in the paper said that the black bear population was on the rise and that several had been spotted by hikers near the Leiber State recreation area and also over at Cataract Falls, neither of which was very far from here.

"Maybe we should get the animals loaded up and get back," Bill said. He was right; they needed to get moving. It was almost two o'clock in the afternoon, and there was still plenty to do, but Mary still wanted to grab supplies from her house.

As they stood around the carcass, Nugget came over and joined them. The little dog was curious and began circling the area with her nose to the ground. Mary was surprised to see how reluctant Nugget was to get too close. On the dog's second pass around the pig, she veered off and followed a scent on the ground, leading away from the carcass. She walked several feet toward the back of the property, sniffing the ground as she went, until she finally stopped and stared off into the field behind them.

"She smells something she doesn't like," Mary said.

"We really should get going." Fred walked over to the horse trailer and inspected it. "What size ball does this take?"

"Two and a quarter inch," Mary answered. "I'm not sure what the Ford has, but I have the right size hitch on my Jeep."

"That's what I have on my truck. I'll tow it," Bill offered.

"I'll help you with the gate." Fred caught up to Bill, who had already started walking back to the truck.

"While those two do that, let's look around the barn and figure out what else we need to take with us." Reese followed Mary back to the barn, and they started gathering supplies that would help keep the animals at the motel. Mary was sure to grab a few hand tools that she used to clean out the barn from time to time. With the animals living that close to them and in such tight quarters, keeping the courtyard as clean as possible would be important. She knew how fast it could get gross, and dirty animal was the last thing she wanted to smell on a regular basis.

They also grabbed what feed she had left in the barn. One of the bags had been gnawed through, as she suspected. It must have been the goats or pigs or maybe a combination of both.

"Hey, look at all these eggs!" Reese was loading a bucket with eggs from the now-empty nesting boxes. "There must be close to twenty here."

Mary smiled. "I bet there's just as many under the front porch."

The thought of fresh eggs for breakfast made her hungry. At breakfast this morning, they had filled themselves with oatmeal, bread, and canned fruit, but they couldn't survive on those types of food for long. They needed more than carbohydrates; they needed protein.

"How long will these be good for?" Reese asked.

"They taste best if you eat them within a couple weeks, but they'll last a month or more," Mary answered.

Reese laughed. "I don't think we'll have any trouble eating these before they expire."

"No, I imagine not." Mary smiled. Even though two of the chickens were unaccounted for, they still had ten chickens and four ducks left. The chickens were pretty regular at egg production, and most of the hens laid one a day. The ducks weren't as consistent, but they usually produced an egg every few days or so.

The duck eggs were more than twice the size of the chicken eggs, though, and they were rich in protein. If Mary and the others rationed them properly, they could each have at least one egg a day, maybe more if they were careful and let their reserves build up.

Reese continued to gather eggs as Bill entered the yard and backed his Dodge up to the trailer. The animals scattered as the loud modified exhaust of his truck echoed off the sides of the barn. Fred closed the gate behind the truck and hurried over to help hook up the trailer to the hitch. Within a few minutes, they were ready to start loading animals. It was time for Nugget to swing into action.

Nugget didn't need any cues from Mary, and she had already started chasing the goats when they scattered from the exhaust.

"Come on, Nuggs. Get 'em!" Mary called out as the little dog worked the livestock around the yard and slowly back to the trailer. Herding was always more fun when Nugget was involved with the livestock to some degree. It also helped Mary catch the occasional stray back when one of the goats managed to escape the fenced-in yard. But this was different, and Mary was proud of her girl for doing what she had been trained to do.

Reluctantly, the animals funneled into the trailer at Nugget's insistence and the occasional nip to their flanks. The chickens resisted the most, and their ability to launch themselves into the air and over Nugget's advances made them all the more difficult to round up. Eventually, the last of the chickens in the yard was corralled into the trailer. Now they just had to catch the ones under the front porch.

After they closed the trailer up, Fred and Bill lingered around the back of the truck for a moment. Mary noticed that they were acting a little odd and wondered what was going on.

"What's wrong?" Mary asked.

"Well, we were just thinking that we should take the dead pig with us, too." Fred cleared his throat and broke eye contact with her momentarily.

Mary sighed and looked back at the dead pig for a second. "Is the meat any good, Reese?"

"She's only been dead for a few hours, as far as I can tell. It's probably still good," Reese answered. Part of Mary had hoped Reese's answer would be no. But it wasn't, and as sad as Mary was to lose one of her animals, she didn't want to let her emotions get in the way of her common sense. She couldn't deny the others meat because of her feelings. She also knew the reality of the situation: the pig would go to waste if they left it out here to rot in the sun. Even if they took the time to bury it, something— maybe whatever had killed it in the first place— would come along and dig up the carcass after they were gone.

"Fine, go ahead and load it up. I'm going to head on up to the house. I'll see you there when you're done." Mary turned and started to walk away. "Don't forget to grab the pile of tools by the barn." She turned and nodded at the items her and Reese had gathered, then went into the house.

"Thanks, Mary. We'll take care of it." Bill tipped his hat as she passed.

"I'll come with you and give you a hand, if that's okay," Reese called out, chasing after Mary and Nugget.

By the time Mary reached the house, she had let her emotions get the best of her and was steadily wiping away tears and fighting off the desire to have a good cry. It wasn't the pig. Well, not entirely. It was everything, and it seemed to all come crashing down at once. Reese finally caught up to her and put her hand on Mary's shoulder.

"I'm sorry…about the pig."

Mary shook her head. "Silly, isn't it? I mean, it's just a pig, right? There are more important things to worry about right now."

"No, it wasn't just a pig. It was an animal that you took care of and cared about. What happened isn't your fault. It's okay to feel bad. You're allowed that much. What's going on around us doesn't make us any less human." Reese followed up her pep talk with a quick hug.

Mary smiled at Reese. She felt silly letting her emotions get the best of her, but Reese made her feel a little better. In some ways, she reminded Mary of her daughter, and it was good to have Reese with them. In fact, Mary was thankful she could draw strength from all of them. And as bad as it was right now, she was still more fortunate than most.

· 23 ·

In a little less than an hour, they had the fourth Suburban loaded onto the trailer and chained into place. Vince was impressed with what they had accomplished, but it had come at a cost: not one of them was dry. The sun was almost unbearable, and even with frequent breaks to hydrate and hide in the shade of the loader, it looked as though they had all gone swimming in their clothes. Whatever water they had consumed wasn't enough to stay hydrated.

Normally the SUVs would be situated with a small amount of space between them for transport. But they weren't worried about delivering pristine vehicles to the motel, so they winched them snuggly together on the trailer until their bumpers mashed into one another.

Doing this allowed them to squeeze a small sedan on the back end. They couldn't fit the entire car on the last bit of ramp, and the rear wheels hung off the back by a few feet and touched the pavement. But the car was front-wheel drive, and Vince hoped it would tow behind without any trouble. To be honest, though, if they lost the car en route to the motel, it wouldn't really matter. It was at least worth the effort to try and take one more car with them. Fortunately, they found plenty of tie-downs on the trailer, and they made sure the large SUVs wouldn't go anywhere while being towed. Although Vince wasn't overly concerned with securing them, it wasn't like they were going to be moving very fast.

He dreaded the prospect of towing the cumbersome and overloaded trailer back to the motel, to say the least. He'd had a little taste of what it was going to be like when he tried maneuvering the trailer through the car lot. They added a few safety chains to the loader bucket and trailer connection to try and ensure a problem-free trip back, but Vince was skeptical. Though the chains wouldn't keep the king pin from sliding off the bucket, they would at least stop the trailer tongue from hitting the ground and getting damaged. That was the theory, anyway.

He was relieved to see the loader lift the trailer with relative ease, considering it was loaded down with five vehicles now. He certainly had his doubts about whether the old John Deere would be able to handle the weight. Once he had the trailer raised high enough for towing, Vince had John and Cy lower the landing gear on the trailer as far as they could without touching the ground. This would provide another safety measure should the pin slip off the bucket.

With every precaution taken, it was time to start the slow journey back to the other side of town. Vince adjusted himself in the seat so he could have a decent view of both the road behind him, which was now the front of the loader, and the trailer. Fortunately, he had a pretty straight shot out of the car lot and onto the road.

John and Cy followed behind in the Bronco and kept an eye on things from the rear. Once again, Vince wished they had an extra radio to keep in touch, but they didn't, so he kept an ear out for John's horn. If John or Cy spotted any problems, they had agreed that they would honk the horn to let Vince know. It wasn't the best plan, but they had little choice in the matter. The horn on the old Bronco wasn't very loud and hearing it over the sound of the diesel was tough enough, but now there was the added whining of the hydraulics, which were now under a load and supporting the weight of the trailer tongue.

Vince felt very isolated in the cab as he carefully transitioned from the parking lot to the street and over a curb he didn't mean to drive over. The trailer leaned precariously to the left and then back to the right as Vince held his breath and watched the vehicles bounce around and test the strength of the tie-down chains. The way they had it loaded made the whole thing top-heavy, but he expected as much since the lower half of the trailer was empty. Watching the vehicles shift their weight from side to side, which in turn caused the trailer to sway dramatically, was still nerve-wracking.

He was glad to reach the somewhat flat surface of the road as he prepared to navigate around the first wreck. In hindsight, he should have cleared the road entirely rather than just push things out of the way. He hadn't anticipated that towing the trailer back would be such a technical endeavor. The articulated steering compounded his every turn of the wheel. Throw in the added complication of doing it all in reverse and just keeping things going the direction he intended made for a formidable challenge.

Vince glanced at his watch and quickly looked back to the road, afraid he would lose control. He was disappointed to see it was almost four in the afternoon. He swore that when he checked the time a little while ago it was closer to three. There was a bit of a learning curve with this first load of cars, and hopefully the others would go much smoother and faster.

For the most part, he was satisfied with how the rig was performing, minus the steering, and the king pin seemed to be happy resting on the piece of steel between the forks. Vince was worried that it wouldn't hold up, but now he was wondering if he would be the weak link in all this. The way he was sitting in the seat so he could see both in front and behind the loader was starting to take its toll on his back. He wasn't sure how many trips he could make like this.

John, Cy, and maybe some of the others would have to take their turn behind the wheel. Vince hadn't planned on doing all the towing, but he didn't think he'd need someone else to take over for him so quickly. He'd hoped to make a few more trips today, but the reality that they might only make it out to the dealership once more began to settle in.

And they had to deal with more than just the cars and the animals. The looters were never far from his mind, and he was sure they were on everyone else's, too. A part of him fully expected to hear the radio go off and warn them that they were under attack while they were at the dealership. John had checked in with the radio on a regular basis, but all was quiet back at the motel. The looters certainly knew by now that the boy was missing, along with several of their people. Whether they had found the bodies or not was anybody's guess.

With five guys and the Lincoln missing, Vince hoped that hiding the bodies would have the looters suspecting their own gang members of foul play and buy them some time. The fact that they hadn't been attacked suggested that this was exactly what was happening. It wouldn't last forever, though, and eventually the looters would figure out what had happened, especially when no supplies were brought out to the overpass.

Vince questioned whether they should even attempt another run tonight. With the load of cars they had, they would be able to lay out a formidable roadblock and movable entrance on the main road into town. It would take them at least an hour or more to unload the Suburbans and put them into place across the road. The looters hadn't specified when they expected the supplies to be dropped off, just that they wanted them tonight.

Vince was almost sure they would have a scout watching the overpass and reporting any activity — or lack thereof — back to the rest of the gang. At a certain point, it would be obvious that Vince and the other survivors didn't intend on giving in and handing over any supplies. There was no telling what would happen, really. The looters had lost their bargaining chip, and if they still thought that some of their own gang members had the boy, they wouldn't want Vince and the others to know that, either.

No matter the outcome, Vince wanted everyone to be ready for battle tonight. That meant putting cars and animals on hold until tomorrow morning.

He hated to stop working on these things, but it wasn't smart to have people spread out all over town when an attack was likely. The looters' mobility would be limited thanks to the damage he and John had done to their vehicles, but that was no reason to let their guard down. Plan for the worst, hope for the best. Vince liked to live by that motto, but now it carried a whole new meaning: the worst was death and the best would be surviving another day.

· 24 ·

John hadn't mentioned if he'd heard over the radio how Mary and her team were making out with the animals. Vince had meant to ask, but they had been working nonstop at loading cars, and it slipped his mind. Hopefully Mary had managed to rescue all the animals from her place and set them up at the motel.

He'd find out soon enough; the motel was less than a mile away. They were almost back, and aside from a few hairy moments when he had ridden up on the curb during a couple of wide turns, the trip had been uneventful. The loader was operating flawlessly, and for its age and appearance, Vince was impressed with its performance. Of course, this also made him suspect that something was bound to go wrong at any minute. Things had gone too easily today, and in his mind, that meant trouble was likely around the corner. He hated that he thought that way, but he did, and given their circumstances, he was getting more cynical by the day.

Vince didn't want to admit it, but he was becoming more and more callus to the plight of other possible survivors outside their group. He had initially hoped they would find more people, but now he wasn't so sure about that. Unless he personally knew someone, he wasn't sure he could trust them to join him and the others at the motel. Not without a healthy amount of scrutiny at the very least. After all, he'd gone against his gut feeling with Dave and Kelly, and where had that gotten him?

He felt a small sense of relief as he passed the motel and waved to Tom, who was sitting in the car on watch. Vince was glad to see him up, and although he wanted him to rest up, taking a watch shift wouldn't hurt him. Besides, it would free up an able-bodied person to help elsewhere, and right now, Vince hoped that someone was making dinner.

He also noticed the black Ford was back, and Bill's Dodge, with Mary's horse trailer attached, was parked along the far side of the motel parking lot. That was a good sign, and it gave him a small boost of energy as he continued toward the old roadblock. He was tempted to stop and see how they had set up the courtyard—and more importantly how many animals had actually survived—but he knew they were losing daylight and he desperately wanted to place these SUVs before tonight.

Vince eyed the overpass suspiciously as he pulled the trailer into place near the roadblock. He scanned the area near the interstate access ramps and the road beyond as best as he could, but the heat rising from the asphalt distorted his view. Past a certain point, he couldn't tell if he was seeing the reflection of an ATV or if it was just the sun glinting off a wreck on the road.

Vince was tired, and after further inspection, he decided it must have been a mirage. He wiped the perspiration from his face and tried to focus one more time before giving up. The sweat stung his eyes, and the yellow glare from the sun was unrelenting, even at this hour. He had wished for clearer skies and less smoke, but now he was rethinking his wish. It was nice to breathe more easily, but he wasn't sure it was a fair trade. At least the solar panels on the garage were getting a solid day of charging.

John and Cy weren't far behind him and pulled up next to the loader. They all went right to work unloading the SUVs without saying much to one another. Vince could tell that they were either tired or worried about what the night might bring as far as the looters were concerned.

At least unloading was easier than loading, and they let gravity do most of the work. They were done in a fraction of the time it had taken them to winch the Suburbans and the sedan onto the transport trailer. Unfortunately, they had to unhook the loader from the trailer so Vince could use the bucket to clear the old roadblock out of the way. The wrecks he moved wouldn't go to waste, though, and he strategically placed them on the shoulder and used them to fill the ditch that ran parallel to the northbound lane.

Using the heavy bucket, he did his best to flatten the cars and push them into the bottom of the ditch until they were about level with the surface of the road. His plan was to use those cars as a base to fill the ditch and then stack more on top of them. He'd do the same on the other side when they had more time and more cars.

While he was setting the wrecks in place, he noticed just how tall the grass and weeds were growing. They were mostly weeds, but it made him think about how there were no more services like road crews or the big orange tractors that he'd seen cutting grass along the local roadways. Vince wondered how long it would take for nature to reclaim what had been paved over. An image of Cloverdale in ruins and overgrown with vegetation popped into his thoughts.

Vince shook his head as if he could throw the image from his mind. He had to stay focused. It had been a long day and the heat in the cab was getting to him. Maybe it was time to let someone else have a turn behind the wheel for a while.

Vince put the loader in park and opened the cab door all the way. "Anybody want to take over for a while?" Cy jumped at the opportunity and was waiting at the bottom of the ladder as Vince climbed down. He tried to explain to Cy how he wanted the SUVs arranged by drawing a small diagram in the crusty dirt, but he wasn't sure if his son understood. Vince had a specific way he wanted this done, so he decided to stay nearby and direct from the ground.

Initially, Vince assumed they would roll the new vehicles into place, but he forgot that they needed the loader to move the old ones. Since they had it unhooked from the trailer, they might as well use it.

Cy carefully scooped up the first Suburban with the makeshift forks just far enough to clear the ground with the tires. He knew it didn't matter, but he felt bad treating the expensive SUV so roughly and he didn't have the heart to tilt the bucket back and mar the glossy paint. Instead he decided to go a little slower and balance them solely on the forks instead.

His dad was waiting impatiently where Cy was supposed to place the truck. But as Cy swung the loader around and came to an abrupt stop before straightening out the wheel, the nearly three-ton SUV broke free of the bucket and slid off the forks. Cy froze as he watched the scene unfold in what felt like slow motion, the vehicle heading straight for his dad.

Vince ran to the left and dove, rolling the last couple of feet to safety as the truck made contact with the ground only a few yards away. Luckily the tires caught on the road with a loud screech and stopped the forward momentum. The Suburban teetered on two wheels for what seemed like an impossible amount of time before slamming back down on all four tires.

Cy's heart was beating so fast he thought it might jump out of his chest. What had he done? He felt horrible for being so careless, and in hindsight, he should have known better. He was exhausted and wasn't thinking clearly. The heat had taken a toll on him and his wits today.

Cy flung the cab door open. "Are you okay?"

John was already standing next to Vince and helped him to his feet.

"Yeah, I'm fine." Vince brushed the dirt and dried grass from his clothes before looking at Cy. "You tryin' to kill me?" He shook his head.

"Sorry, it...it got away from me." Cy felt about three inches tall.

"If you don't want to work anymore today, just say so. I can take a hint," Vince joked.

Cy was glad to see his dad was okay and willing to make fun of his mistake, but it did little to settle his nerves.

Cy began to climb down. "Somebody else better run the loader."

"Nonsense. It could have happened to anyone. Don't let it beat you," Vince insisted.

Cy paused halfway down the ladder. His dad was right; he always was.

"You sure?" Cy asked.

Vince nodded. As Cy climbed back into the cab, he remembered a time when he was little and wrecked his go-cart while racing around his family's property. He'd managed to take out a good section of fencing along the house in the process. That day, he had wanted to hang up his racing gloves forever and sell the go-cart to help pay for the repairs. But his dad insisted that he get back on and ride around until the feeling passed. His dad had always been that way, and although it was tough to go along with at times, it always worked out for the best.

Cy eased the bucket into place and slid the forks back under the Suburban. He only had to move it a few more feet, and he was relieved to finally set it down and back away.

When he picked the next one up, he didn't hesitate to tilt the forks back and cradle the SUV properly, like he should have the first time. This one was silver and looked every bit as nice as the last one. It slid down the forks and landed against the bucket with a crunch, but Cy didn't care this time. These overpriced SUVs were only worth as much protection as they could provide when used for a roadblock. He couldn't believe he had almost killed his father because he didn't want to scratch the pretty truck.

Cy shook his head as he maneuvered the loader to the next spot. This wasn't a game they were playing. Not that he ever thought it was, but the close call made things seem much more real. If one of them were injured beyond what Reese could patch up, there was no one else to help. And based on how things were going, that wasn't going to change anytime soon. They were truly alone out here, and everything they did had consequences.

· 25 ·

Vince continued to direct Cy from the ground. His nerves were still a little rattled from the near miss, but he did his best not to show it. He needed Cy to move past the mistake he'd made. The last thing his son needed was to have his confidence undermined right now. There was no place for that in this new world.

Vince knew it was a slippery slope, and once you lost confidence, it was only a matter of time until your ability followed. He'd seen it before in the field: hesitation or a lack of certainty could result in a man's death. And the situation they were in right now wasn't any different or any less deadly than some of the worst he'd seen in his career with the army.

With all four Suburbans in place Vince walked around the new roadblock to the Cloverdale side, inspecting their creation as he went. With two of the long SUVs blocking the left and right shoulder and the other two blocking the north- and southbound lanes, the road itself was impassable.

The Suburbans on the road were offset behind the other two a little so they could be pushed or pulled out of the way, effectively creating a movable gate into town. They could work out the best way to do that later, but for right now, nobody was going anywhere.

Vince checked his watch and then glanced at the westbound sun. It wouldn't be totally dark for a few hours, but they were going to lose the good light soon. The air might have been cleaner, but the yellow haze had not diminished any, and it seemed to cause the light to fade faster than normal as the sun closed in on the horizon.

Cy approached in the loader, carrying the smaller sedan, and waited for Vince to show him where he wanted it. Vince had him place it tightly against the Suburban on the northbound shoulder. This was also the same side he had put the wrecks in the ditch. The sedan neatly covered the distance between the last Suburban and the ditch itself, ending just on top of the wrecks.

This was the first real piece of their wall, albeit a very small piece, and for the first time, what Vince had imagined was turning into a reality. They had a long way to go, but he was happy with how much they had increased their security just by doing this little bit. This was only the beginning, and now that they knew the drill, Vince hoped to add many more vehicles to the wall in much less time.

Vince, John, and Cy stood there for a minute, admiring their efforts, before Cy broke the silence.

"Are we doing more tonight?" he asked. Vince looked at John, who shrugged.

"I'd like to," John answered, "but I'm worried we may get some visitors."

"Same," Vince agreed. "And I don't think we have time to get another whole load in before dark." They could work in the dark, but that meant they'd have to use the lights, which could give away their position to the looters.

He thought about at least taking the trailer back to the car lot tonight before calling it quits, but the longer he considered the plan, the less he was inclined to run it back. Besides, making it a temporary part of the wall wouldn't hurt. He didn't want to risk damaging it, but it could serve as a safety if the looters did attack and were crazy enough to try and ram their way through.

"Do you think they'll show up tonight...for the supplies?" Cy asked. "I mean, they don't have Ryan."

"Hard to say what they'll do," Vince said. "There's no way they got all the vehicles repaired in this short amount of time."

"I agree, but I wouldn't count them out," John sneered. "They're gonna be real butthurt over what we did to 'em. They will want revenge, make no mistake about that."

"We'll be ready for them," Vince said.

The truth was, they weren't ready for them, not entirely. Vince and the others were more prepared for an attack than they had ever been, especially with the new roadblock in place, but they still had a lot to do. They needed to finish the wall, and Vince needed to figure out how to run electricity to the motel so they could all enjoy a few modern-day conveniences and maybe feel human again. That would go a long way toward improving their level of preparedness and ability to fight. While he worked on the power situation, he wanted to run lines to a few strategically located spotlights along the barricade of cars as well. Being able to light up the looters when they attacked would be a huge advantage.

He also still wanted to make it out to his house and salvage what he could from his gun safe and possibly anything else that had survived. After the ride out to the dealership today, he had resigned himself to the fact that his house was a loss. Seeing the ratio of surviving homes to destroyed homes, he realized that the odds of his house not being burned to the ground were extremely low, and he decided it was best not to assume otherwise.

Even though there was still a long list of things to do, he felt good about what they had accomplished today. It wasn't a lot, but it was a start, and it proved that they could do it. They had ventured into the ruins of town for the first time since the EMPs and moved forward with their lives. Now, if only Mary and her team had found some animals and set up a pen at the motel, the day would be complete in his mind.

John and Cy had returned to the motel ahead of Vince. He was eager to see how Mary and Reese had made out today, but first he wanted to use the loader to put the trailer into a better position for the night. It wouldn't take long, and then he'd be right behind them.

He'd also left a spare key to his garage with Mary so the ones who stayed behind today could refill the water containers, something he hoped they had actually done. Vince looked forward to a fresh jug of semi-cool water all to himself. Not only was he hungry, but he was parched as well. The last few bottles of water he drank were warm and not exactly refreshing.

With the trailer in place, Vince ran the loader back to the motel and parked it in its usual spot along the curb. Tom was still on watch and made his way out of the Lincoln when he saw Vince coming.

"Looks like you guys did pretty good today," Tom called out before Vince had climbed all the way down from the cab.

"Yeah, it went all right, I guess. We'd hoped to make a few runs, but there's always tomorrow." After jumping the rest of the way to the ground, Vince stretched his arms above his head. Knowing he was done with the loader for the day felt good.

"How's the arm?" Vince asked.

"Not too bad." Tom attempted to lift his arm a few inches off his body but struggled against the restrictive bandages and sling. Reese had fashioned them out of a cut-up towel to keep his arm immobile. Tom winced a little as he let it back down.

"Well, don't push yourself. Let it heal and do what Reese tells you. You're still a big help just standing watch. In fact, maybe you could take more watch shifts if you're up to it."

Tom nodded slowly. "Sure, Major. I guess I could do that. Don't worry, though. I'll be back in action in a few days."

"Don't rush it. You need to heal properly," Vince cautioned as he started across the parking lot for the motel. It would take a couple of weeks before Tom was healthy enough to help out with what needed to be done around here. Vince wasn't blaming him, even though it was Tom's fault that he got shot, but he just wanted to be realistic in his expectations. If standing watch was the only way Tom could contribute to the group, then he should do that as much as possible.

"You should see how they got the animals set up," Tom called out as Vince continued across the parking lot. "They did a real good job with that today."

"I'll be sure to take a look," Vince answered.

Vince was reminded that he had the 12:00 to 4:00 a.m. watch tomorrow morning, and he wanted to talk to John and Cy about that. If he was already going to be up, he might as well head over to the garage after his shift and get to work on a way to run power from the solar panels to the motel. There was no reason why John and Cy couldn't handle a few runs to the dealership on their own. It would be easier if they started early, anyway, before the heat could slow them down.

The mornings were always cooler, and Vince also considered them the least likely time for an attack. They should be taking advantage of the lower temperatures, and after struggling with the oppressive heat this afternoon, he was going to suggest that they all work more in the early morning hours from now on. The heat had taken too much out of them, and he felt they could have accomplished much more if they didn't have to take so many water breaks. They might even have to consider sitting out the middle part of the day if this heat wave continued.

· 26 ·

Vince hoped they could try and return to some type of normal schedule—or at least as close to normal as possible. The extra rest they all enjoyed and then grew sick of when they were trapped in their rooms for the first few days had long worn off. Everyone had the same look on their faces: total exhaustion. Between the rescue mission and crazy hours they were keeping, no one had gone to bed at a decent hour lately.

An earlier bedtime was one of Vince's goals for tonight, especially since he had to get up so early for watch duty. He thought about how good it would feel to take off his boots and lie down tonight, but as he neared the motel, he smelled something that made him forget all about how tired he was.

He couldn't put his finger on the delicious aroma that filled the air, but his mouth began to water just the same. He wasn't sure what they were making for dinner tonight, but it was undoubtedly the best thing he'd ever smelled in his life. Other than a protein bar and water, he hadn't had anything since their late breakfast this morning, and his stomach growled with every step he took toward what had become their dining room.

Vince was about to open the office door and follow his nose to dinner when he stopped and noticed that the vending machines and ice machine had been moved. With the promise of food, he'd forgotten all about the animals. He ignored his grumbling belly and wandered over to take a quick look at the courtyard. Approaching the section of fence that extended from the ice machine to the exterior of the motel wall, he leaned over the makeshift barricade to see how Mary and the others had set up the courtyard. He counted the animals but gave up when he got to the chickens, which were constantly on the move and chasing bugs as they pecked at the ground.

"Quite the petting zoo, huh?" Mary surprised him; he hadn't noticed her walk up behind him.

"Looks like you guys had a pretty good day."

"Bill and Fred followed Reese and me out to my place with his Dodge. We made a pretty good haul today."

Vince smiled. "I can see that. Great job."

Mary joined Vince at the gate and leaned over. "That's only half of it. We also brought back all the preserves from my basement, along with a few other things. We made two trips out there today."

"Wow, I'm impressed." Vince paused for a moment as he looked the animals over. "Aren't you missing a pig?"

Mary lowered her head, and he suddenly felt bad for asking so casually.

Mary shrugged. "Yeah, one of the sows didn't make it. She was attacked by something."

"I'm sorry." Vince put his arm around her and tried his best to comfort her. He wanted to ask about what she meant by attacked and if they knew what had done it, but he didn't want to risk upsetting her further.

"It's okay. I'm over it." She leaned into him a little. Vince wasn't buying her claim of being over the loss of the pig, but he figured it was best to let it go.

"Oh, I don't know if you want to get that close. I'm a little ripe," he joked.

She laughed. "Aren't we all?"

"I plan on doing something about that. Going to get started on that effort tomorrow morning first thing." Vince straightened up off the fence and was suddenly aware of how disgusting he felt.

"Oh, by the way, here's the key to the garage. Everything is off and locked back up." Mary fished around in her pocket, but Vince stopped her.

"Why don't you hang on to that, just in case?" He shrugged. Mary smiled and they both watched the animals for a second.

"Well, come on. Dinner is just about ready, and I know you're starving. I'll see you in there in a minute. I'm going to go knock on some doors and let the others know. That's what I came out here to do in the first place." Mary put her hand on his shoulder as she headed off.

Vince really was pleased with the courtyard setup and gave it one more glance as he walked away. They'd all worked hard today as well. It had taken a lot of effort to accomplish all this. Just the watering trough alone must have taken a while to fill, what with all the trips back and forth to the garage to fill containers. The animals would go through a lot of water in this heat, and that was just another reason to get the water working at the motel.

Vince was proud of his little group, and he felt hopeful that everything was going to work out. Cloverdale would never be what it once was, but it would be something again—they wouldn't be wiped off the map forever. And if they could survive, then there had to be other towns that would make it, too.

When Vince entered the room, Sarah and the kids were setting the table for a proper sit-down meal. They had even gone so far as to set up a folding table in the corner so that everyone had a decent place to sit. Both tables were complete with tablecloths and candles burning at the center of each one.

"Wow, lookin' good in here, guys," Vince said.

"Wait until you see what's for dinner. Be right back." Sarah's eyes widened and she disappeared through the large swinging door leading to the kitchen. Ryan and Sasha remained behind, laying out silverware rolled in paper towels at each setting. Then they took seats at the smaller folding table when they had finished.

"What's for dinner?" Vince asked the kids.

The two of them looked at each other until Sasha finally spoke up.

"Meat soup." She covered her mouth and giggled.

Vince wasn't sure what that meant exactly, but if it tasted half as good as it smelled, he didn't care. The others slowly trickled into the room and everyone took their place around the tables. Within a minute or two of everyone settling in, Sarah and Beverly emerged from the kitchen with an oversized steaming pot and a tray of buttered bread.

The ladies made their way around the table with the pot and served everyone a healthy portion of soup before having a seat themselves. Vince used his spoon to stir his bowl and was surprised to see something that resembled a normal meal. There were potatoes, corn, beans, and zucchini, along with large chunks of ham.

Of course, the missing pig. Now he had even more questions about the attack and what happened to the animal, but he didn't want to bring it up right now, not in front of Mary. She looked like she was having enough trouble dealing with the bowl in front of her. She smiled and joined in the conversation, but Vince knew her well enough to know that this bothered her.

The animals Mary had on her little farm were all rescues, taken in from people who either didn't want them anymore or couldn't keep them for one reason or another. They weren't livestock to Mary; they were pets. Not a pet in the way that she thought of Nugget, but close. They all had names, and Vince was sure that made this all the more difficult for her. He watched her as she picked out the vegetables and ate them along with the bread. When she had finished, she put her bowl down on the floor and let Nugget eat the chunks of meat she had left.

They all wolfed the food down, and as soon as Beverly was done, she announced that she would go and relieve Tom so that he could come in and enjoy the meal like the rest of them had. Everyone else chipped in and helped clean up—except for Mary, who excused herself and said she was taking Nugget outside for a bit. When Vince carried the large pot into the kitchen, he knew why she hadn't wanted to help out with the clean-up.

There on the large stainless-steel island in the middle of the kitchen was the remainder of the pig.

"I did the best I could. Butchered plenty of deer but never a pig." Bill had quartered the animal and done a decent job of it in Vince's opinion.

"Reese estimated it had only been dead for a couple hours or so and that the meat was still good. We couldn't let it go to waste," Bill added.

Vince looked the meat over. "I see you've got it salted up pretty well."

"Yeah, Mary had a bunch of salt in her basement for canning and pickling, so I figured we could cure the meat and keep it from spoiling. I even grabbed some empty feed bags to wrap it up in. We can keep it in the walk-in for tonight. It's not cold, but it's probably cool enough to keep it till morning with the salt on it."

"Yeah, that's a good idea, but we'll still need to figure out where to keep it long term," Vince said. Having this meat was a big deal, and it would feed them for a while. He hated that it was hard on Mary, but this was too good of an opportunity to waste. It benefitted the greater good, and that was how they had to think of things now, even though that wasn't always the easiest thing to do. Vince and Bill further discussed how to best preserve the pork quarters while they helped clean up.

Eventually, they decided that the best thing to do was to dig an old-fashioned root cellar. For the time being, burying one of the empty fifty-five-gallon plastic drums Vince had sitting in his garage might be enough, but eventually they would build something more permanent.

Behind the motel, there was a massive mound of dirt left over from when they had cleared the property many years ago to build the place. It had long since been forgotten and was grown over with grass and a few small trees. They could easily dig into the side of the hill with the loader and create a root cellar. There was certainly enough scrap material lying around to line the cellar with wood and build a well-insulated door to close the whole thing up tight.

Not only could they keep the meat longer, but they could also store any vegetables they harvested or anything else they wanted to keep cool and preserve. It was one more job to add to the ever-growing list of things to do, but it would be worth the effort. This wouldn't be the only meat they had to preserve. At some point in the future, they were going to have to hunt game to survive. The eggs would go a long way toward providing them with a source of protein, but they needed variety, and any meat they could hunt or catch would help their canned goods last longer.

Vince and the others had been busy worrying about what they needed right now, but they needed to consider more than just their immediate needs. It was time to start thinking about long-term sustainability and how they could prepare for the hardships that were sure to come. There was no telling when or if help would ever come. And even if help did come, it would most likely be too late to matter if they didn't take action now.

It was hot now, but cooler weather would come in a few months. Then winter would set in. Vince thought about the freezing-cold days he'd spent in his deer stand last hunting season and how good it felt to come home to a nice warm house with the woodstove going. Life wasn't going to be that easy anymore. The stakes were higher now, and the days of hunting for recreation were over.

Now, if they didn't get a deer or a turkey or whatever they were hunting, they might not eat. There would be a whole new set of challenges to deal with in the days and months ahead, and they would surely test their endurance as a group.

Find out about Bruno Miller's next book by signing up for his newsletter:
http://brunomillerauthor.com/sign-up/

No spam, no junk, just news (sales, freebies, and releases). Scouts honor.

Enjoy the book?
Help the series grow by telling a friend about it and taking the time to leave a review.

ABOUT THE AUTHOR

BRUNO MILLER is the author of the Dark Road series. He's a military vet who likes to spend his downtime hanging out with his wife and kids, or getting in some range time. He believes in being prepared for any situation.

http://brunomillerauthor.com/

https://www.facebook.com/BrunoMillerAuthor/

Made in the USA
Monee, IL
24 June 2021

72177765R00111